what we keep
is not always what will stay

For Tony and the original Felix

what we keep
is not always what will stay

AMANDA COCKRELL

Woodbury, Minnesota

First Edition
First Printing, 2011

Cover design by Kevin R. Brown
Cover images: Day of the Dead figure © iStockphoto.com/Luis Sandoval Mandujano;
      heart © iStockphoto.com/Artur Figurski;
      bow © iStockphoto.com/Donna Coleman

Flux, an imprint of Llewellyn Worldwide Ltd.

Library of Congress Cataloging-in-Publication Data
Cockrell, Amanda.
  What we keep is not always what will stay / Amanda Cockrell.—1st ed.
    p. cm.
  Summary: Fifteen-year-old Angela, distraught over her mother and stepfather's separation, confides in a statue of St. Felix that suddenly seems to come alive, after which she befriends Jesse, a nineteen-year-old disabled veteran, although Felix, her family, and friends warn her to be wary of him.
  ISBN 978-0-7387-2615-1
  [1. Interpersonal relations—Fiction. 2. Family problems—Fiction. 3. Veterans—Fiction. 4. Amputees—Fiction. 5. People with disabilities—Fiction. 6. Saints—Fiction. 7. California, Southern—Fiction.] I. Title.
  PZ7.C6472Wh 2011
  [Fic]—dc22

                        2010054517

Flux
Llewellyn Worldwide Ltd.
2143 Wooddale Drive
Woodbury, MN 55125-2989
www.fluxnow.com

Printed in the United States of America

(

I am not a religious fanatic. I want to say that right off. It's just that ever since I got lost looking for the bathroom at church when I was little, and found a statue of St. Felix down in the basement, I've talked to him.

He's down there because we aren't supposed to pray to him, since he's one of those saints the modern church thinks might have been just a product of somebody's imagination, which is embarrassing if you've been asking him to intercede with God for you. But he looked, I don't know, friendly. Like someone I could tell things to. I'm fifteen now and I've been talking to him since I was nine. He's life-size, and has gray hair and a gray beard and a kind of white gown with maybe a red and blue cross on the front, but he's really faded and you can't tell for sure. The name

"Felix" is carved into the base, by his feet. I looked him up in a *Lives of the Saints* book and I think he's Felix of Valois, but he might be one of the other Felixes—there have been lots, some of them even more dubious than Felix of Valois. Nobody knows where the statue came from. It looks hand-carved, and some early parishioner probably made it. Nobody pays any attention to him now. I dust him once in a while, while I talk to him.

He's like having a diary in invisible ink. From my lips to his ear, as my grandfather says, and no one can ever read what I've written. I told him when Noah Michalski tried to put his hand up my shirt at a church dance and then told the entire planet I'd *let* him, which I hadn't; and when my cat died; and when my mother decided she was going to divorce Ben, who's a perfectly good stepfather that I've had since I was eight.

"Ben says Mom will come around," I told Felix. I leaned against the dusty old wall and picked paint flakes off it. There was more dust dancing around in the light from the window over his head, like an extra halo. "Mom gets like this every summer," I told him. "Like she wants to migrate or something, and then she settles down in the fall. But I don't remember her ever being this bad." Usually she just goes to Big Sur for a week and writes poetry. Mom teaches English at Ayala Middle School, where they all think she's terribly cool because she has this head of wild red hair and wears arty clothes. I look a lot like her, except for having dark hair and my dad's Latino coloring, but for some reason all that wild hair that looks arty on her just looks dorky on me.

"I told Mom that Ben is the nicest guy I know," I said to St. Felix. "And she said you can't stay married to somebody just because they're nice."

St. Felix looked sympathetic. I flopped down on the floor at his feet, poking with a finger at his carved sandals. "I remember when they got married. I was the flower girl. I had a big basket of rose petals." I looked up at St. Felix. "People are supposed to hate their stepfathers. I *like* Ben. He'd probably have adopted me if we could have found my real father and proved he's dead. You'd think my mother would want to set me a good example. How am I supposed to find a boyfriend with an example like that?"

I poked at his sandal some more. "I haven't spoken to her since she said she was leaving Ben and we had a big fight over it. I don't know how long I can hold out. It's not easy not talking to your mother." It felt good to tell someone that, even a statue, since I couldn't say it to Mom if I wasn't speaking to her.

———

And then, the next day, Mom moved out and went to my grandparents' house. For a whole week now she's been calling and pestering me to move there with her. I'm still living at Ben's. Ben's house is where I've lived since I was eight, and I'm not going anywhere. I've managed to hold out not speaking to Mom, too pig-stubborn to say one word to her when she tries to talk me into going to my grandparents' house. Then she orders me to come, then threatens to call the police and have them *bring* me there. I'm mad, but I'm sort of enjoying how nuts it's driving her.

She finally came over here to argue about it some more while Ben and Grandma Alice and I were having dinner. Grandma Alice is Ben's mother, and she moved in with us last month, not long before Mom moved out. Grandma Alice offered to move out again but Mom said that wasn't the problem, she would rather have Grandma Alice than Ben. She said it right in front of him, but he just grinned at her. Grandma Alice says there may be things I don't know.

So Mom walked into the dining room as if she'd never left and started talking to me while I was buttering my potato. "Angela, I am your mother, and I will make the decisions as to what is best for both of us. You need to stop behaving in this childish fashion."

No, I don't, I thought. *You need me to.* I cut my potato into tiny little bites, which Mom hates because she read somewhere that it's a sign of an eating disorder—which I don't have, but which she thinks I might develop at any moment, like a pimple on my nose.

"Sylvia," Grandma Alice said, "maybe it's best to let Angie have a little time."

"No reason she can't stay here," Ben said, spearing another piece of steak.

"Of course she can't stay here," Mom said.

I got up while they were arguing and took my plate

to the kitchen, and then went out the back door before Mom noticed. I figured I could get several blocks away before Mom got around to wondering why I was still in the kitchen.

Our house—well, Ben's house—is right downtown. It's not much of a town. There's only one stop light. I ducked under the big live oaks that shade the library and jaywalked across Ayala Avenue to my church, St. Thomas Aquinas. It isn't one of the famous California missions that Father Serra founded, but it's almost as old. I like it lots better than the new church Mom goes to. It's always cool and dim at St. Thomas's, even if Mom does think it has mice. It smells like incense, and the adobe walls and the stations of the cross are all dark from the candle smoke.

It was dusk when I headed out and St. Thomas's was dark inside, just the glow of the candles in the chapel that people light to thank the Virgin for something, or to ask her to keep their husband safe in the army or make him faithful or let them win the lottery. I skirted by them, thinking maybe on the way out I'd light one for Mom to get some sense.

The stairs down to the basement are gloomy; they always make me think a nun is going to pop out at me wearing one of those old-fashioned habits, or some ancient padre from the colonial days will dodder past, speaking Spanish, but there's never anyone down there. As I reached the bottom step, I saw St. Felix in the light from the one little high-up window. He looked tired, and kind of gloomy too. Whatever he was wearing looked like the mice had gnawed it, and it was more faded than ever. I felt around for the light switch and turned it on. St. Felix looked back at me and scratched his beard, and I screamed.

"Oh, hell," he said. "I didn't mean to scare you."

"Who are you?" I backed away.

"Felix." He pointed at his feet. "It's on my pedestal."

I stared at him. I could have sworn it *was* St. Felix. He had on this sort of white bathrobe thing, and sandals—Birkenstocks, I think. His hair was gray and sort of shaggy like Felix's. And he stepped down off St. Felix's pedestal, and there wasn't anybody else on there.

"There's all kinds of people upstairs," I said. "People come down here all the time."

"No, they don't," he said. "But I'm not gonna hurt you. Are you still fighting with your mom over the divorce?"

"How do you know that?" I demanded.

He looked hurt. "What? You think we don't pay attention to people who pray to us? It's not like I have lots of people down here, lighting candles and gilding my halo."

"You don't have a halo," I told him.

He felt around in the air over his head as if it had just gone missing. "Hmmm. I expect they don't manifest well."

I knew I was probably trapped in the basement of St. Thomas's with a lunatic, but where had the statue gone? "You aren't St. Felix," I told him.

"I'll prove it." He sat down on a wooden box labeled NATIVITY, ODD PIECES. "For starters," he said, "do *not* hang around with that Michalski boy. All that fifteen-year-old boys have on their minds is getting in some girl's underwear."

I could feel my face going hot. It's one thing to tell something like that to a statue; it's another to have the statue turn into a live actual man.

"Second, your mom is divorcing your stepdad and you don't like that. And, three, you got *nice* hair."

Oh, God. I remembered telling him when I got my first period. He was a *statue*. Then.

It was halfway a relief when it occurred to me that all the things he was talking about were stuff I'd told him recently. "If you're St. Felix, what's my father's name? Not Ben, my real father."

My mother gets married and divorced when she hasn't got anything else to do. She married her first husband, whose name I don't even know, when she was sixteen, but her parents had it annulled. Lots later she married my father in a nuptial Mass, which didn't work any better than the Las Vegas wedding had because all Mom got out of that marriage was me.

"Gil Arnaz," Felix said.

I tried to remember the last time I had talked about Gil Arnaz. It *might* have been while I was talking about the divorce. I edged past him to look around the broom closet door, which was standing half open. A ratty old blanket and a backpack were on the floor with an empty can of spaghetti. There was probably enough room to sleep in there if you took out all the old mop buckets and moth-eaten cassocks, which somebody had done.

"You've been listening to me!" I said.

"Well, sure. You've been talking to me."

"I've been talking to St. Felix!"

He smiled. His teeth were snaggly. "It was nice. Nobody else has talked to me in a long time."

"You're not St. Felix!"

He pointed a finger at me. "If I'm not, then where is he?"

"If you are, how come you're suddenly alive?"

He looked like he was actually trying to figure that out. "I guess God finally decided I wasn't a saint."

I rolled my eyes.

"On the other hand," he said kind of thoughtfully, "it gets real hard to be a saint when somebody's trying to kill you. I think God was expecting too much. What do you think?"

"I think if Father Weatherford catches you down here, he'll call the police."

"Are you going to tell him?"

I absolutely did not believe this man was St. Felix. And in any case, nobody ever tried to kill St. Felix of Valois, who led a very boring life at his monastery—although he once found the Blessed Virgin and her angels in the chapel ringing the bells for him when he overslept.

"I can ask God to change your mom's mind about the divorce," the guy said. "I don't think he actually listens to me, but if you want me to, I'll ask."

I pictured myself telling Father Weatherford about him. I'd have to explain about the statue being gone and why I'd been coming down here and I'd sound like those people who see the Virgin Mary in a cheese sandwich. Before I could make up my mind, I heard someone walking around upstairs in the chapel, which has a tile floor. I ran up the stairs and out the side door, and left St. Felix to fend for himself.

———————

Mom was gone by the time I got back. Grandma Alice and Ben were in the kitchen scraping plates and giving bites off their forks to the Todal, who is a giant dog named for the monster in *The Thirteen Clocks*, which was Mom's favorite book when she was little. The Todal was the size of a calf when we got him, when he was ten weeks old. No one knows exactly what he is. He leaned against Ben, looking soulful and hoping for the rest of my potato.

"The coast is clear," Ben said. "Where'd you disappear to?"

"Just out for a walk." I didn't feel up to telling anyone about the guy in the church basement. Mom would freak if she knew, and want me to carry mace, and Ben would probably call the cops. I didn't think the guy was dangerous, though. I know that's stupid, to assume some random man who's been sleeping in the church basement and claims he's a saint is harmless, but I did anyway. I'll probably be abducted by aliens before I'm twenty.

Ben was watching me, looking worried. He's more worried about me than he is about Mom, I think. It drives me crazy that he's so casual about her leaving—does he *want* her to divorce him?

"Have you started getting your stuff for school together?" he asked, reminding me that there's less than a month of summer vacation left, a dismal thought. "Backpack and everything? Do you need new clothes? Do we need to shop?"

"Have you considered the possibility that Sylvia will go ape if you take Angie shopping?" Grandma Alice asked him.

"I can take myself," I said. "I can take the bus to Ventura." Ayala only has one department store, where you can buy things that look like they came out of the *Farmer's Almanac.* I absolutely did not want to go shopping with Mom, and I couldn't picture Ben hanging around the Juniors section in Macy's.

Ben frowned at the bus idea.

"I can go with Lily," I said. "She just got her license." Lily is my best friend.

"Does Lily have a car?"

"We can take her dad's." I slid out of the kitchen and into my room, hitting Lily's number on my cell. I had it on silent, and I'd stacked up five missed calls from Mom since dinner.

———

"People get very strange over custody issues," Lily said seriously when she picked me up the next day in her parents' old Volvo.

"It's not as if Ben could get custody," I grumbled. "She's just freaking because I won't talk to her."

"You'd be freaking if she wouldn't talk to you," Lily pointed out.

What I like about Lily is that she takes everything seriously, even though she can be a goof. She never tells me I shouldn't do something, she just makes what she calls "suggestions," and when I do it and it turns out to have been a disaster, she never says she told me so. She also has absolutely straight blond hair that she winds up into a knot and sticks a pencil through, and it stays. I don't know how. Mine is a mess of curls and it still won't do the pencil thing. Lily is sixteen already, but she's in tenth grade with me because her parents lived in a monastery in Nepal until she was seven and they just never got around to putting her in school there. They're a little casual that way. Her family moved to Ayala when we were in middle school and we're both such weirdos that we were destined to be friends. Neither of us has any clue how to deal with people our own age since we're both only children and were raised by wolves. Arty, intellectual wolves.

"Ben gave me his credit card," I told Lily. "I don't think it's even an account that Mom's on. That'll make her mad, too."

"Are you trying to make her mad?"

"Mmm hmm."

"Constructive." Lily swung the Volvo around the corner.

When she stopped for the light by the post office, I

saw him. It was St. Felix of whoever-he-was. He was walking from St. Thomas's toward the Spanish-style arcade that runs through Ayala's one-block shopping district. He was still wearing that old bathrobe thing, but I could see he had jeans on under it.

I poked Lily. "Who's that?"

"Someone who's not taking his medication?" she suggested.

We watched him go past the drug store, the bathrobe flapping around his legs. Lily turned the Volvo left and forgot about him, but I craned my neck around to see if I could see where he went.

We spent the afternoon trying on clothes and counting up how many people we know whose parents are divorced, which was depressing.

"Okay, count how many aren't," Lily said, inspecting a pair of khakis in the three-way mirror.

"Yours aren't. That's one." I pulled a too-tight shirt back over my head. I have Mom's shape, which is top-heavy. Tank tops that look great on Lily, who is thin and ethereal, make me look like a hooker. On the other hand, I have good legs and a perpetual, non-cancer-inducing tan. I piled my hair up on my head to see what it would look like and decided it made me look like Chiquita Banana.

"Yours aren't yet," Lily said firmly. "You have to figure out *why* she wants a divorce. Then you'll know what you're up against."

"She doesn't have a reason," I said. "As far as I can tell."

"Trust me. She does."

"There's got to be something I can do. If I was in a sit-com, I would. Courageous, sensible teen shows parents the light."

"There's a philosophy for you—TV as a guide to life."

"Or I could consult a psychic." That would work about as well as anything else I've tried so far.

Lily took my hand and stared at my palm. She crossed her eyes. "I see tall dark stranger, many lovers, career in moving peectures," she said in a really horrible accent.

"For Mom? That's what I'm trying to prevent."

"No. For you. Take mind off. Also ice cream."

A double-cherry/coffee ice-cream-cone fix only lasts thirty minutes, but it's great while it's working. I also swear I saw Felix again, with a cone in his hand, while Lily was backing the car around.

2

It's a lot harder to think someone away than it is to think them up. I avoided St. Thomas's, even on Sunday, but after that night I started seeing St. Felix everywhere. I saw him in the park at Bowlful of Blues, talking to a woman selling batik jackets. I saw him at Domenico's Pizza washing out garbage cans. I saw him in Safeway buying cigarettes. Each time, he smiled at me but didn't say anything. He was always wearing his old white bathrobe over jeans and a T-shirt. Nobody ever seemed to say anything about that.

On the other hand, Ayala is used to practically anything. The Theosophists started a foundation here in the 1930s and they imported peacocks that run wild all over the East End now. All kinds of Hollywood people live here—big celebrities, not just people like Ben, who's a screenwriter. Mostly we're polite and pretend we don't recognize them. Plus there are all the tourists and the acupuncturists and aromatherapy shops and pet psychologists. So, given all that, maybe a guy in a bathrobe isn't worth commenting on.

The time I saw him in Safeway, I almost gave him the no-smoking lecture, since he'd already butted into *my* life. Maybe he could tell—he smiled again and slid behind a shelf of soup, and I didn't see him again for a few days. I even began to wonder if I was nuts and he really didn't exist, especially when I mentioned him to Lily and she didn't remember him. Then, just when I thought he was a figment of my imagination, I saw him having coffee with my mom.

They were at Bert's Used Books, under a eucalyptus tree at a table by the cash register. Bert keeps everything except the best books on outdoor shelves, with little fiberglass roofs over them in case it rains, which it hardly ever does. The guy had his robe on, and his backpack was under the table by his feet. He was talking, waving his hands around, and Mom was listening, her fingers under her chin and a little smile on her mouth.

I just stood there between the science fiction and the mysteries and gaped at them, and then I took off before they saw me.

I hung around outside, cruising the twenty-five-cent shelves by the sidewalk where if you want something after hours you throw a quarter through the fence. When Mom came out, she was by herself. I let her get a little way down the block and then I ran after her.

"Mom! Who is that guy?"

She jumped when I grabbed her arm, and then she glared at me. "I thought you weren't talking to me."

I gave her what she calls *that look*, as in *don't give me that look*. "Who is he?"

"He's ... I met him in the history section at Bert's. He's just someone I have coffee with."

"Why?"

She gave me back the look and then she sighed. "Angie, you really don't have the right to question me like that."

"What's his name?" I demanded.

"Felix."

"It's not."

"Why shouldn't it be?"

I opened my mouth and closed it again. "He's creepy," I said.

"He's had a rough time," my mom said. "He has post-traumatic stress disorder, I think."

"You mean from a war?"

"Probably. He just wants someone to talk to. And so do I. Things aren't easy right now."

I thought about saying that was *her* fault, and then I thought about Grandma Alice saying maybe there were things I didn't know. Mom says you should never start a relationship with someone whose troubles are greater than your own. She should know. I just hoped she remembered that right now.

"You weren't at Mass on Sunday," Mom said, dodging the issue.

"Didn't feel like it," I muttered.

"Feeling like it isn't the point."

"Anyway, how do you know?" Mom goes to Our Lady of Good Counsel, the new church.

"Wuffie told me."

Wuffie is my grandmother—Mom's mother—but one of those grandmas that don't want to be called Grandma and instead pick out something like Wuffie or Foofoo, so they sound like you got them at the pound. Wuffie still goes to St. Thomas's, and I should have known she would rat me out.

"All right, I'll go next week," I said.

"Good. Well…" Mom hesitated, as if she expected me to say something else, but I couldn't think of anything that didn't sound petulant.

"Ben misses you," I said.

Mom sighed. "Oh, honey, sometimes you can't make things work the way you want them to." She sounded less angry and sadder than she had in front of Ben. "Well. Well, I'd better go. I left vegetables in the car." She raised her hand as if she was going to hug me and then turned it into a sort of wave. "See you." She turned and walked down the block to her car. Her red hair made a wild cloud around her head, bobbing along behind her as if it were alive. I ran my fingers through my own hair and discovered I had a eucalyptus bud stuck in it.

The next day I looked for Felix and didn't see him so I went back to St. Thomas's. I had some idea I'd find the statue in some back room there, and the guy's stuff all over the basement floor because it was obvious he wasn't really St. Felix. I was right about all of it but the statue. The pedestal was still sitting there with nobody on it. I poked around in the various closets and storage rooms and found old brass altar vases and a stack of hymnbooks that mice had chewed, but that's all. Except for the guy, who was sitting on the floor by the pedestal, mending a frayed cord on a hot plate. He jumped when I came in, and looked relieved when he saw it was me.

"They'll catch you," I told him. "There are shelters you can go to."

"I like it here."

"Why were you at Bert's with my mom?"

"Your mom?"

"Looks like me. Lots of red hair. Don't say you weren't."

"That's your mom? I was interceding."

"You weren't."

"I was working up to it. I will now, if you want."

"I want to know where the statue went. That was *my* statue."

"I don't know," he admitted. "I don't know how it happened. All of a sudden, here I was."

"It did *not* happen like that," I said, furious.

He looked like he was trying to remember. "It might have," he said finally. He bent his head over the cord again.

The sun was coming through the window at the top of the stairs, leaving a little pool of light at the bottom. I sat down on the last step. "You know, that stuff I told St. Felix was private," I said.

"Everyone has secret lives," he said. "Everybody running around with all kinds of horrors inside."

"Well, not horrors…"

"No, not you. Think about that and how that means you're one of the lucky ones. Not like that kid who used to be in your mom's class, the one she was telling me about."

"Who?"

He bent his head over the cord. "He went to Afghanistan and got his leg blown off the first week. He got out of the hospital yesterday."

"His leg? Who?"

"I don't know. She didn't tell me his name."

———

"His name's Jesse Francis," Mom said.

I'd called Mom when I got back to Ben's. Ben was in his study, and Grandma Alice was washing lettuce in the sink.

I remembered Jesse Francis. Ayala is a small town. "He's barely old enough to be in the army!" I said to Mom. "What was he doing in Afghanistan?"

"His father signed for him to join when he was seventeen." Mom knows nearly everybody whose kids she's taught. "It's such a hard age, seventeen," she said quietly. "And how did you hear about it?"

"Some of the kids," I said. I wouldn't have to pretend—something like that would be all over town. When I looked down at the *Ayala News* on the table, it was on the front page. His truck had been blown up by an Improvised Explosive Device, which is what they call a homemade land mine. It blew his whole leg off. I could feel my stomach contracting into a knot.

Grandma Alice pottered in with the place mats. "Awful," she said when she saw the paper. "Set the table, okay?"

I put the phone back in the kitchen and got plates. At dinner Grandma Alice lit the candles and said a blessing because it was Friday night. She and Ben are Jewish and so is Mom's dad, my Grandpa Joe, but Mom and Wuffie both got some kind of special dispensation to marry them, and agreed to raise the kids Catholic. That's okay with me. I figure that with a background like that, you either have to be an atheist or just pick something. And I wouldn't be a good atheist. The idea of random chaos is too scary.

Grandma Alice made matzoh ball soup with homemade chicken broth. I would be Jewish just for matzoh ball soup, but tonight at first it felt like eating lead slugs. Or real ones. I didn't know Jesse Francis, not really. He dropped out the year before last and he's four years older than me. But all I could think of was what it would feel like to have your leg explode. After dinner, I went back to St. Thomas's and slipped down the stairs.

"You were right," I said to Felix. "How could they let a seventeen-year-old kid volunteer to go to Afghanistan?"

"Same way they always have. Wars are fought by kids. Kids are who's expendable." He looked really sad in the light from the one dusty bulb.

"His *father* signed so he could go!" I was indignant. "How could somebody's father do that?"

"He thought it was the patriotic thing to do." Felix's face had gotten closed up, like a cupboard someone had locked.

"How do you know?"

"I know."

I sat down on the stairs again. I hated to admit it, but it was kind of nice having him talk *back* to me. And weird. I found myself wanting to say things to him, as if he really was St. Felix. Maybe Mom felt that way about him. I didn't like that idea much. "Mom is going to get back with Ben, you know," I said.

He looked up at that. "Yeah, probably."

"That hot plate will blow the fuses here," I told him. "This place has wiring that's really scary."

"You know about wiring?"

"Wuffie got my Grandpa Joe to come look at it, and that's what he said."

"Is your grandpa an electrician?"

"He's a history professor, but he's retired."

Felix smiled then. "We all want to fix stuff we don't understand."

I had to laugh. "Grandpa Joe exploded a toaster once."

"I'll try not to explode the basement. You figure God's got his eye on it, he'll put the fire out?"

"I hope so," I said.

Walking back to Ben's in the dark, I wondered how much God really keeps an eye on things like that. I got the feeling that there were layers of things I couldn't see, floating on top of each other. Maybe it was the live oaks. They have strange gnarly branches and are mostly really big and old. They look like something might be living in them—dryads or something, not just owls. Once I saw a peacock in one. The Chumash, the people who lived here in the valley before the Spanish came, lived on the acorns. They believed their dead people went away over the Channel Islands off the coast in a blue light and you could hear the door of the Underworld banging closed behind them if you listened. I wondered if that was what the explosion had sounded like to Jesse Francis.

———

On Sunday I went to church because Wuffie came and picked me up. At least she hasn't tried to get me to come live with her and Mom. She doesn't approve of the divorce, either.

It was the Sunday before Labor Day, and Father Weatherford was dedicating the Mass to the new school year to get us off on the right foot.

"There's someone living in the basement here," I said to Wuffie as we settled in our usual pew.

"I know, dear," she whispered back. "Your mother told me."

"*She* knows? And you haven't said anything?"

"Poor man. I think Father Weatherford may know, but the parish council won't like it so he pretends he doesn't. But haven't you noticed how *clean* everything is?"

I hadn't, but now that I looked around, I could see that someone had painstakingly cleaned all the separate panes in the stained glass windows. You have to do that with a Q-tip to get the edges. And the statues of the Virgin and St. Thomas looked brighter. The Altar Society at St. Thomas is all old ladies; their eyesight isn't that good and they can't reach the tops of anything. Father Weatherford won't let them use a ladder for fear one of them will fall off and break her hip. I imagined Felix cleaning those little glass panes one by one and wondered how long it had taken.

———

After church, Lily and I had plans to go up to the river to swim. About twenty people were holding a peace vigil in front of the park when we drove through town. They were just standing there with anti-war signs. The hardware store across the street had a big flag banner and a bunch of yellow ribbons in the display window, and the manager was standing outside, glaring at the people with the signs.

"Did you know Jesse Francis?" I asked Lily.

"Not really."

"Mom says he's coming back to finish his senior year of high school. How weird is that?"

"That's beyond weird. High school would be like living on Mars after you'd been in the army, I'd think. Didn't he already get his GED?"

"Mom says Jesse's mother told her he just sits in his room and draws mazes in his journal and she's hoping that if he goes back to high school he can figure out how to be a kid again."

"Man, I doubt it," Lily said.

"Yeah, I don't see how you could either. But Mom says colleges like to see a diploma and not a GED, and that's why he decided to go back."

"And I thought you weren't talking to your mom."

"We have negotiated the terms of a truce," I said. "She doesn't try to get me to live at Wuffie's house and I don't nag her about Ben."

"If she actually gets divorced, *that's* going to get a little bizarre."

"Yeah. Mostly I'm hoping it means she's not really going to go through with it."

"Is she seeing anybody else?" Lily asked.

"She has coffee with a homeless guy who lives in the basement at St. Thomas's. I don't really think you can count that."

"No," Lily agreed. "You can't count that."

I hoped you couldn't. When we got to the river, the swimming hole was full. Some kids we knew were climbing up to jump off the big tawny rocks that jut out over the water. We kind of half waved at them—one of them was Noah Michalski—and spread our towels out on the bank. Lily waded in and I followed her, pushing out into the cool water. It was too murky to see the bottom, but it's over your head in the middle. Lily floated on her back with her pale hair spreading out around her, waving its tendrils in the current. A shower of manzanita leaves drifted down on my head and I looked up to see Noah Michalski hopping up and down and making ape noises.

"Mature," I said, and he just laughed. Noah is really cute, but he's an idiot. He has blond hair and green eyes and a sort of Superman curl over his forehead, and all he thinks about is sex and exploding things. He acts like he still likes me. I can't imagine why, because I told him I wouldn't spit on him if he was on fire. When I fall in love it will be with someone I can trust, not someone who will trash me to make himself look like a stud. And then I won't leave him for some stupid reason like Mom keeps doing.

I flopped onto my back like Lily and closed my eyes, just drifting on the surface of the water, paddling with my hands a bit now and then to keep from floating downstream out of the pool. A bunch of little kids were running up and down along the bank throwing gravel on each other. I could smell somebody else cooking hot dogs. The sky was that bright robin's egg blue with the sun not even thinking about going down behind the mountains, as if it would stay up there all summer, and summer wouldn't end.

3

But on Tuesday of course we were in school—so much for never-ending summer. At least I'm not going to the school where Mom teaches anymore. I'm looking forward to buying Twinkies from the vending machine without getting a long, soulful discussion about healthful eating. On the other hand, in middle school we were the big kids, and now we're back to being at the low end of the food chain. I was pleased to see that Noah Michalski isn't looking nearly as cocky as usual, either.

Lily elbowed me. "Isn't that Jesse Francis?"

Jesse Francis looked like someone had taken the kid from the paper and overwritten him entirely with someone else who just looked like him. He was tall, with dark hair cut short and an Adidas jacket that might have belonged to him before he went into the army. He had on baggy khakis and you couldn't see which leg was missing, but from the way he walked, I thought it was the left one. He looked not quite balanced, as though he was still learning to use the artificial leg. He had a pink piece of paper in his fist and was peering at it as if it might be in code. Everybody made a little space around him. Finally he said to a senior, "Hey man, where's the Multipurpose Room?" and the senior pointed.

"That's what they renamed the cafeteria last year."

"Thanks, man." Jesse nodded and headed that way, while the senior stood looking after him as if he had just talked with somebody famous or scary or both. A bunch of senior girls stared at him as he went by, too, and went into an Urgent Discussion Huddle as soon as he'd turned the corner.

By the time we found our homeroom and got our schedules untangled and had lunch, the day was pretty much over. None of the teachers ever expect to get anything done the first day. Lily's in most of my classes and we both have Drivers' Ed, even though Lily already has a license. Drivers' Ed is what you take in the tenth grade no matter what. I wonder if they're making Jesse Francis take Family Living with the rest of the seniors. That's the class where they have them carry a raw egg around all day and pretend it's a baby.

——————

Turns out that Jesse Francis is in my art class. He was sitting by himself on the first day, folded up on a stool with his elbows on his knees. The studio is about half student desks and half stools at the work table. I was late and everybody else had dumped their bookbags and stuff into the empty seats and no one looked inclined to move their stuff for me, so I climbed up on the stool next to Jesse.

He gave me a grave nod. He has huge dark eyes under dark brows and his skin looks like it's stretched just a little too thin on his face. I nodded back.

Mr. Petrillo, the art teacher, said that we were going to do freehand sketches of this apple—he held it up—just to get limbered up. So we did that, while he walked around the room looking at our apples.

"Nice line … think *shape*, remember, this thing is round … don't try to photograph it, child, loosen up … you, too, it's not a blueprint …"

I snuck a look at Jesse's apple. It looked as if he had drawn it without ever lifting the pencil off the paper, just run the point around and around some real apple that wasn't visible to anybody else.

"That's really cool," I whispered. "How did you do that?"

He shrugged. "It's just a trick."

Mr. Petrillo liked it. He pinned it up on the board as one of the ones that had captured the essence of apple.

"What are you doing in beginning art?" I whispered.

He shrugged again. "I needed an elective." He kind of smiled. "It's better than marching band."

"Oh my God, I would think so," I said, and then thought that might not have been the best thing to say. But he cracked a smile.

"The leg makes me walk funny." He lurched his shoulders from side to side like Frankenstein.

I didn't try to pretend not to know what he meant. Everybody in school knows, and he knows they know. "And the uniforms are dorky," I suggested.

"And the uniforms are dorky."

"Angie, a little more attention to your drawing, please," Mr. Petrillo said.

We didn't talk anymore that day, but the next day when I saw him in the hallway, he grinned at me and gave me a little wave. I was kind of flattered he remembered me. Then at lunch we saw him sitting at a table by himself, a stack of books at his elbow, reading *Modern U.S. History* and eating soup out of a microwave cup. He still had that sense of empty space around him. I saw a couple of boys head for his table and then sort of bend around it at the last minute like they were being deflected by some kind of invisible force field. The only other person eating lunch by himself was the D.A.R.E. officer. I raised my eyebrows at Lily. We hadn't staked out any lunchroom turf yet, and don't really belong to any recognized group.

"Sure." Lily hefted her tray and we plopped down across the table from Jesse. He looked surprised.

"We'll go away if you want," I said.

"Why do I want you to go away?"

"We're just sophomores," Lily said.

He kind of smiled. "What's your name? I know this one." He nodded at me.

"Lily Reinder."

"Reindeer?"

Lily rolled her eyes. Everyone always does that. She spelled it for him.

"I'll just call you Rudolph."

"You've got soup on Dwight D. Eisenhower there," Lily said.

He glanced down at the book and picked a noodle off the page. He'd doodled a little wandering maze pattern all around the border of the picture.

"They'll charge you for the book if you write in it," I told him.

"Looking out for me?"

I could feel my cheeks go hot. I must have sounded like a doofus, about twelve.

"It's okay, I probably need somebody to," Jesse said.

I thought maybe he did. I could feel the gaggle of senior girls at the next table giving us the X-Ray Vision stare, but none of them had sat down next to him.

Something made a huge bang and a thump and we all jumped. Not that there isn't enough noise in the cafeteria to rattle hell already, but this was not a usual noise. I stood up on my chair because everybody else was standing up too, but I still couldn't see. Mrs. Richardson, the principal, was pushing her way through the crowd with an exasperated look on her face, and the D.A.R.E. officer was putting down his cheeseburger. The big trash can with the swinging lid that sat by the kitchen door was on its side, and there was gunk everywhere—with Noah Michalski sitting in the middle of it, chili running down his ears. The bang had apparently been the can going over with Noah in it. A little red-haired junior was staring at the garbage on her khaki skirt like she was about to cry, and two senior boys were looking around as if they had just happened to be by the trash can at the wrong time and hadn't really tried to stuff Noah in it on a dare.

Noah's face was bright red and he looked furious. He jumped up and shouted something I couldn't catch, except for the words "blow you all away—" And that's when all hell broke loose. The D.A.R.E. officer snapped to attention and grabbed him by the arm. The fourth period bell went off, and then the fire alarm bell on top of that, and then there were campus security cops all over. Someone started giving totally unintelligible instructions over the intercom. I climbed off my chair and saw that Jesse was flat on the floor, under the table.

"Line up!" someone yelled. Jesse didn't move. I bent down and shook him, and his face was pure white when he looked up at me. He got to his feet and lined up with the rest of us without a word, and we all marched out into the parking lot. There were sirens going off now, and cop cars rolling into the lot, and we all stood around waiting for someone to tell us what to do next, and speculating.

"It's a bomb threat."

"Nah, that kid had a gun."

"Someone pulled the fire alarm."

"Dude, I swear, a gun—I saw it."

Jesse had some of his color back. We were standing under a pepper tree at the end of the lot. He leaned back against it and exhaled slowly while a Channel 10 News van rolled by us.

"Are you okay?" I asked him.

"Oh, Christ. I didn't think I would do that."

"Do what?"

"Hit the floor like a fool. I thought it *was* a bomb." He looked around us carefully, like he still wasn't sure, but he said, "Now everybody will know I'm a headcase."

"Considering it's Noah, it might have been a bomb," Lily said. "He got suspended last year for blowing up one of those big cans with a cherry bomb."

"It wasn't his fault this time," I pointed out. "Those seniors started it." And then Noah, of course, being Noah, had to say something stupid and send everyone into a panic.

Exciting stuff gets around a small town fast. Car after car was pulling into the lot, and the school rent-a-cops were stopping them and trying to tell them nobody had been shot, but the cars were full of parents and they weren't listening.

"Nobody was paying attention to you," I said to Jesse. "They were all too busy gawking at Noah."

He shrugged. It hunched his shoulders up like a bird sitting in the rain. "Doesn't matter." But he looked like it did. "My shrink says I'm not supposed to worry about what people think. I was there, and they weren't. I'm me and they're not." There was a tic beside his right eye. He shot a glance at Noah and said, "Asshole."

That was when Ben and Mom showed up, at the same time in separate cars, and screeched to a halt right next to each other.

4

"Angie!" Mom flew over to me. Her hair looked like an explosion, some kind of alien shrub, and she kept pushing it out of her face.

"It's okay, Sylvia," Ben said. "I got her. You need to get back to class."

Mom turned away from me and glared at him. "And how exactly do you know what I need to do?" she asked, while I stood there totally mortified, hoping the ground would open up under them, not me.

"I assumed that you were in class," Ben said to Mom. "You always are, this time of day." He gave her that reasonable look that he uses when they fight because he knows it drives her nuts. "I can be more flexible, so I figured I'd better come get Angie."

"Angie is not going home with you!" Mom snapped.

"I live there," I said.

"We'll talk about that! Oh never mind, I'll take you back there for now."

"Who's taking care of your class?" Ben asked her.

"Not your business! I'm just as capable as you are of being *flexible* when my child is concerned." She grabbed me by the arm.

"Okay, now I can't ever come back here again," I said as she towed me to her car. "Maybe when I'm forty-five. I might live this down by then."

Mom's lips were pressed together and she was really pale, like she might throw up. "Angie," she said, "just be quiet."

"Are you taking me to Ben's?" I demanded as we got into the car. I wouldn't put it past her to kidnap me and drive me to Wuffie's.

Mom started threading her way between all the other cars trying to get in or out of the lot. There were three cops in a huddle, but no one was directing traffic. "Yes," she said after a minute, between her teeth. "I'm taking you to Ben's."

I took a good look at her then. "Mom? What's wrong?"

She took a deep yoga breath and let it out again.

"Don't close your eyes," I said. "You're driving."

"They said there was a shooting," she said carefully. She still looked like she was about to puke, and I realized she'd been scared to death, not just mad at Ben.

"It was just some morons having a fight." I tried to sound soothing.

"With guns?"

"No guns. Honest." We turned the corner onto Signal and I said, "It was cool of Ben to come get me."

"He is *not* your father!"

I wanted to say, *he ought to be.* He's absolutely an improvement on my actual father, who just went off and forgot all about me. But I thought better of it. I thought maybe she was rattled enough that I might get some information out of her, though, so I said, "Why are you so pissed off at him? Not about him coming to get me. I mean, pissed off enough to divorce him."

She took another deep breath. "That is not your business."

"It is so! Don't you think I *care* who I live with? How do I know *what* moron you might marry next?"

"I am not going to get married again, believe me."

Well, I didn't. She's already done it three times, and at least two of them on the spur of the moment, including the one to my father. Wuffie says he was a gangster. On the other hand, Wuffie thinks most of my friends are gangsters, even though it's just the clothes. So I don't know. Mom says my father knew some scary people and he's probably dead by now. She says it like that's the reason she divorced him, but now she's divorcing Ben, who is absolutely respectable. Why can't she *stay* with someone?

"What did he *do*?" I asked her again.

"He stole something that was mine."

"Stole something?" I couldn't see Ben stealing her money. He makes way more than she does. Had he been wearing her underwear? Maybe I could convince her that transvestites are just normal guys, except for that. Doctor Phil says so. "What kind of something?" I asked, edging up to it.

"Something I told him."

Oh.

"He put it in a script. I told him something private and he put it in a Goddamned movie!"

"Did you ask him to take it out?"

"Yes, I asked him to take it out!"

"You mean he wouldn't?" Unfortunately, I can believe that. We know a bunch of writers besides Ben and I would believe that of any of them. One of them actually put his girlfriend's hemorrhoids into a script.

Mom parked the car in Ben's driveway and jerked the parking brake up. "He said nobody would recognize it and it was *good*. It was just what he needed."

"Um. Well, what was it?"

"I'm not going to tell you!"

"I'll find out when the movie comes out." If it does. The death rate for scripts in Hollywood is huge. We know writers who have made a living for years and none of their scripts have actually been produced. Producers buy scripts and then abandon them, like somebody who buys too many purses. I don't know where all the money comes from.

"I'm sick of the movie business," Mom said. "It's inhabited by shallow creeps. I work myself to death trying to teach kids to speak actual English and everywhere we go, when people find out what Ben does, they latch onto him and I might as well be the housekeeper." She glared at the house as we pulled up, although Ben wasn't in it. "And for that, on top of it, I'm paid practically nothing."

"Would you really *want* to work in Hollywood?"

Mom ran her hands through her hair and then dropped them onto the steering wheel. "Honestly, no. But it's the principle of the thing. And then he had the nerve to tell me my novel needs work."

"He writes movies," I said. "They blow up cars and save the world in a hundred and twenty minutes. Does he really know what he's talking about?"

"I doubt it," Mom snapped.

Grandma Alice came out of the house wiping her hands on her apron and waving a spatula. "I just heard on the television," she called. "They're sending everyone home from all the schools!"

"Oh, Lord," Mom said. "I'd better get back. It's going to be chaos there, too. Honey, call me tonight, okay? If you really want to talk about this, I will, but you won't change my mind." As soon as I got out, she backed down the drive. I saw Ben pull in as she turned the corner; he must have been lurking behind the oleanders, waiting for her to leave.

I thought about cornering him and trying to get him to tell me what he'd put in the script, and to take it out, but I figured he probably wouldn't do either one. And if he *did* tell me, Mom would go postal. So I just focused on calming him and Grandma Alice down, promising there hadn't been any guns, and let it go for now.

Ayala High School was all over the news. We ate dinner in front of the TV while the cameras showed bomb-sniffing dogs and everything, not finding any bombs. The sheriff made a statement and Mrs. Richardson the principal made a statement and Noah's mother made a really furious statement about the sheriff and Mrs. Richardson. I called Lily and she said her parents had been freaked, too, which really isn't like them. They're pretty laid back.

"There's been so much of this stuff," Lily said. "People going crazy and blowing strangers away. So everybody overreacts. That's what Dad said, once he found out it was just Noah Michalski mouthing off."

"But how do you know when it's just Noah, and when somebody just like Noah has gone nuts?" I asked. That's the part that secretly worries me. How can you *tell*?

We analyzed it all some more, and then Jesse Francis of all people called me right after we'd hung up.

"You okay?" he asked.

"Yeah. How about you?"

"Yeah." I couldn't tell if he meant that. But it was extremely cool to have a senior call me and check up on me.

I called Mom, too, but I didn't hound her about Ben yet because I knew she was still mad.

"How was everything at school?" I asked her.

"Madhouse," she said. "Parents having hysterics in the halls. I could wring Noah's neck."

"It wasn't all his fault," I said, to be fair.

"I know Noah," Mom said. "I used to know somebody just like him."

"Who?"

"Long time ago," she said, in a tone that told me not to ask, and hung up in a hurry.

Hmmmmm.

———

Noah got suspended, but not actually arrested because he didn't actually do anything. Mrs. Richardson called an assembly to tell us all that this was an excellent example of what happens when you make poor choices, as if life is a multiple choice test and one of the options is *Make a bomb threat in the cafeteria.*

I thought about talking to Felix about how Jesse hit the floor like that, but figured it might encourage him if he's still seeing Mom. But the upshot of the whole thing is that no one paid much attention to Jesse Francis for a while. Now that it's all settled down again, he's just somebody you pass in the hall, not the Freak of the Week. Lily and I eat lunch with him every day. We've bonded into a cafeteria trio. I think he likes it that we treat him as if he's still a high school student and don't ask him stupid questions like did he kill anyone. All the kids he went to school with his last year here are in college now, or have gotten married and have babies and jobs. They don't cross paths much with people who're still at Ayala High carrying eggs around in their pockets.

They *did* made Jesse take Family Living; he showed me his egg. Sometimes you have to wonder who decides this stuff.

"I was thinking maybe I'd get a hollow one," he told us at lunch. "I think my mom has some plastic ones left over from my brother and sister's baskets last Easter. I could get one of those little corn snakes they sell in pet stores and put it in there, and let it hatch when Ms. Vinson comes around to check them."

"Oh my God, that would be totally cool." I stared at him with admiration—you have to like a mind like that. "You have totally got to do it."

"Nah," he said.

"Why not?"

"It would have been funny when I was seventeen," he said.

"Um." So now he thought I was immature. "So, when you're nineteen, you just think stuff like that up, but you don't actually do it?"

"Life is calmer that way."

Lily said, "When my dad was in college, he put a frog in a salad bowl at a fraternity party."

Jesse snorted.

"My mom yelled at him and put the frog in her purse and took it back to the river. That's how they met."

"I've got to tell Ben," I said. "That's a 'meet cute' if I ever heard one." Movie people are always trying to think up adorable ways to get their romantic characters together.

"Be my guest," Lily said. I couldn't help thinking

about whatever it was my mom didn't want him to use. It's bound to be worse than frogs in the salad.

The bell rang and I groaned; Driver's Ed right after lunch is not a great idea. Mr. Howser always starts us off with a gruesome car wreck video to get us in the right frame of mind.

"Before next week, I have to drive two hours with Mom or Ben," I said, rolling my eyes. "Driving with Lily doesn't count—it has to be with an adult."

"I'll take you out," Jesse said to me. "The 'adult' just has to be eighteen. I remember. We can take my egg for a ride."

"Both of us?" I asked.

"Sure. I can borrow my mom's car. It's an automatic. The only thing I can't handle with the damn leg is a stick. How about it, Rudolph?"

"You bet," Lily said. "My dad talks about our dependence on fossil fuels the whole time I'm driving. I don't know why he doesn't just sign off the hours, but he's overly honest about things like this."

Jesse nodded. "Outgrew his frog period. It happens."

So we all went driving on Saturday and had such a blast. We went out to the East End where there isn't much traffic, and Jesse handed the car over to me. I was a little nervous because it was his mom's car and what if I ran it into a tree?

"Want some music?" he said while I put it in gear.

"Yeah."

He turned the radio on and we all sang along to everything while I drove.

I did all right, though, and when we came to where somebody must have been having a party because there were lots of cars parked along both sides of the street, Jesse insisted I practice parallel parking.

"She's awful at it," Lily said, leaning between us from the back seat. "And we don't know these people."

"All the more reason to practice on them," Jesse said. He showed me how to line the car up with the car in front of my space, and then just when to cut the wheel back over, and I actually got it in the spot without backing into anybody.

"Atta girl!"

He had me do it twice more until he decided I had the hang of it. After that we drove all over the East End, and Lily got her driving time in too, and we ended up going for pizza at Delmenico's. Lily and I had decided beforehand that we would take Jesse out to thank him, and we weren't going to let him pay for any of it.

We started to sit at our usual table at the front window, but Jesse pointed toward a booth in the back.

"What do you like?" I asked him when we'd settled in.

"Pizza." He grinned.

So we ordered our usual garbage pizza with everything on it, and a pitcher of root beer, which, it turns out, Jesse shares my secret passion for. Lily doesn't care what she has to drink as long as she gets pizza. Her parents are vegetarians—they don't insist on Lily being one, but pepperoni and sausage are not household staples for her.

"Oh my God this is good." Lily took a huge bite and pinched the cheese strings off with her fingers.

"You guys are the most," Jesse said. "I can't get over it, you taking me out for pizza."

He sounded like he thought we were cute, and maybe about five, but I didn't care.

"Nobody ever took you out for pizza before?" Lily asked.

"Not for a long time," Jesse said. He looked sad. His face can change in a heartbeat, so that he looks like somebody else.

"You've been neglected," Lily told him. "We'll adopt you."

———————

I like adopting Jesse. He's funny and he knows stuff, not just because he's older, but stuff that no one at school is interested in. Like, for instance, why the oaks look like something might be living in them.

We were working on decorations for Homecoming out of leaves and papier maché. He was making a face out of his leaves, sticking them on wet papier maché and smoothing them down so it looked like a tree person's face.

"That's way cool," I said.

"He's the Green Man," Jesse said. "He's really old. He's from Europe, but I imagine he lives here, too."

"What does he do?" I asked. "Live in the woods?"

"He *is* the woods. He's one of those pagan things the church spent a lot of time stamping out, and then they just gave up and turned him into the harvest festival."

Around here there are lots of overlapping layers of belief like that. This time of year, the people from Mexico go to the cemeteries right after Halloween and clean up the graves and put marigolds and candles on them, then they have a picnic and tell their ancestors the news. They call it *El Dia de los Muertos*, the Day of the Dead. The church calendar calls it All Souls Day. Grandpa Joe says it's because the Aztecs believed death and life were really part of the same thing, and that this is the time of the year when the borders between the worlds are thin. The Church adapted that, the same way it made room for Easter eggs and Christmas trees. People make altars on the Day of the Dead, and put all the stuff their dead relatives liked to eat and drink on them. They make skeleton decorations and dress them up, and if you're a little kid you get a sugar skull with your name on it, just like you would a chocolate Easter egg.

"Got a date for Homecoming?" Jesse asked me, smoothing a leaf onto the Green Man's nose. Homecoming is on Halloween weekend.

"Nah. I'm too weird."

"You aren't weird," he said encouragingly. "You're artsy."

"Are you gonna go?" It was nice that he thought I was artsy.

"Can't dance," he said. "And I'm weirder than you are."

"I guess I could go with Lily," I said. "Lots of girls go

stag. But that felt kind of stupid in middle school, so I think it would feel double stupid here."

"And you're too old to trick-or-treat." He shook his head and looked sympathetic.

"Yeah. Lily and I went last year, but we got a lot of dirty looks."

"Want to come with me, to take my little brother and sister?"

"Is this the booby prize? Are you feeling sorry for me?" I asked.

"Nope. I just don't want to take the little monsters by myself."

"Are you going to wear a costume?"

"No, but you can."

I grinned at him. "What kind of get-up would embarrass you the most?"

"Can't embarrass me." Jesse looked like he was daring me to try.

"Can Lily come too?" It wasn't fair to abandon her on Halloween.

"Reindeer? Sure."

5

I spent some time trying to think up a good costume, and finally settled on La Llorona, who is a famous weeping woman in Mexican folklore. She wears a long black dress and mantilla, and drowned either her children or her husband in the river. Every night she goes back to the river, and either looks for them or drowns them again. There are a lot of variants in folklore.

"'Long Black Veil,' very cool," Jesse said when we knocked on his door, adding yet another variant to the possibilities. Lily had on reindeer antlers. "This is Angie and Rudolph, guys," he said to the two little kids who were waiting with their plastic pumpkins. "Angie and Lily, this is my mom and dad."

His parents shook hands with us very formally and

his mom smiled. "It's nice of you to help Jesse take the little ones out." She tugged at Jesse's pant leg where it was bunched over the artificial leg. "You won't walk too far?"

"He'll be fine," his dad said. "He's supposed to walk."

His mom shot him a look. "In your judgment. Which I have learned not to trust as blindly as I used to."

"Come on, guys." Jesse shooed the little ones out the door. They had masks on but I assumed Batman was his brother and the princess with the wings was his sister. "I hate it when they do that," he said.

Lily gave him an appraising look. I'd told her what Mom had said about Jesse's dad signing him up. "Are you the oldest?"

"Yeah." He lowered his voice. "They had a kid after me, but he had one of those genetic diseases and he died when he was a baby."

"Oh man, I'm sorry," Lily said.

I wondered how much awfulness one family could take. His mom might have had her limit.

Jesse said, "They had a lot of testing before these two. That's Michael under there, and this is Sarah."

"I'm Batman," Michael said.

"And I'm *Princess* Sarah."

"Good wings," Lily said. "I'll trade you for my antlers."

"Princesses don't have antlers. Except unicorn princesses."

A lot of kids were out in the first dark, escorted by parents and older sisters, their flashlights making little circles of gold light. Most of the houses had their porch lights on, so the kids were going to get a good haul.

"Come on, guys. Loot," Lily said, beckoning Michael and Sarah toward the first house.

"Mom's had a rough time," Jesse told me while they went up to the door. "I wish she wouldn't snipe at Dad, though. The army was my idea."

"I guess she can't snipe at you," I said.

Michael and Sarah came bouncing back down the walk and we went on to the next house. Lily was prancing and making what were supposed to be reindeer noises. Jesse chuckled. "She's really getting into it."

I saw that he wasn't walking as fast as Lily and the kids, so I slowed down to match my pace to his. He noticed, and grimaced. "Mom's right. The leg hurts me, but I hate it when she fusses."

I thought it was hard to tell when being nice stopped and fussing started. And how much was it okay to talk about it? "Will it get better?" I asked. "I mean, will you get to where it doesn't hurt?"

"Supposedly. I'm supposed to get another one that's even more high tech. I already feel like a robot."

"High tech?"

Jesse stopped and pulled up his pants leg. I don't know what I was expecting. One of those pink plastic legs, I guess. This one ended in a real-looking foot—I could see it under the cuff of his sock—but the rest of it was made of metal and looked like it could take off on its own.

48

"I can get one that'll let me run marathons. Or play tennis. Or snowboard," he said. "If I did any of those things."

"You might."

"There's a computer in the knee. You tap your toe three times or whatever, and it changes modes. My counselor at the vet center told me about it. It's called a C-Leg." He let his pants leg fall as Lily and the kids came running back.

"Look! We got Snickers!" They took off again.

By the time we'd crisscrossed the neighborhood, their pumpkins were overflowing. Lily insisted we get in her car and go over to the Arbolada, where she said the candy was even better.

"Mom won't let them eat this much candy as it is," Jesse said.

"We can take it to the battered women's shelter tomorrow," Lily said. "It's the principle of the thing."

Batman and the princess were jumping up and down, so he said okay. Lily had extra bags in the car (Lily is always prepared) and we drove across the valley. The Arbolada is an old neighborhood full of big oaks and winding streets with no sidewalks, but no one ever drives very fast, so it's okay. We could see lots more flashlights and hear shrieks and laughing. Lily parked the Volvo next to the old cemetery. It's a little scruffy-looking, with wrought iron fences around it and tall marble angels and obelisks. There are even Civil War veterans buried in it. The little kids grabbed Jesse's hands, one each, and power-walked on past it.

"Good choice," I said.

"Adds to the ambience," Lily said. "You want them to have the full experience."

The white stones looked shiny and ghostly in the moonlight. I wondered if I had any ancestors in that cemetery. Lots of people in the valley are descended from the old Spanish land grant families, like Wuffie, who was a Camarillo. I thought maybe this year I should come out with a vase full of marigolds and some spray cleaner and see if there are any Camarillos there. Wuffie probably wouldn't approve—she thinks celebrating the Day of the Dead is morbid and/or sort of countrified—but my father might have been from Mexico, or maybe his parents were. I feel entitled to that much of him, at least.

Once we were past the cemetery, Michael and Sarah let go of Jesse and followed Lily, who said she knew where the best houses were. Jesse and I ended up sitting on a rock at the end of someone's driveway, waiting for them. I could tell the leg was hurting him but he wasn't going to say anything else about it, so I developed a blister on my foot. I don't think he believed me, though.

But I could see the tension in his jaw loosen up when we sat down and he stuck his bad leg out in front of him. "You look nice in that veil," he said. "It suits you."

"It makes me feel like Zorro's girlfriend."

He reached over and tucked it around my chin, arranging the folds. "Nah. Duchess of Alba."

"Who?"

"By Goya. Famous painting. She reminds me of you."

"Really?"

"Yeah." He smiled at me. "She's always been my favorite."

I can absolutely get into the idea of looking like a famous painting.

After a while, Lily and the kids came back with their bags overflowing. Jesse looked sort of horrified—there was enough candy to keep two little kids sick for a month—but Lily, it turns out, had already negotiated the deal with them and they were all pleased with themselves for collecting candy for the shelter. We sat in Lily's car while they dumped it all out onto the back seat and graded it, putting their favorite stuff back into the pumpkins. They were half asleep and sticky by the time we dropped them off.

"Thanks, you two," Jesse said as he hauled them out and put the princess over his shoulder. "'Night, Rudolph. 'Night, Duchess."

Lily raised an eyebrow, and I said, "Famous painting." A little smugly, I expect.

"Goya," Jesse said. "You should look her up."

So I did, the next day after school. She actually does look kind of like me, and she definitely has my hair. I also looked up the C-Leg online. The manufacturer's website has a picture of the leg, which looks like something you'd see on the cover of a science fiction paperback. It said the C-Leg is "ideal for people who currently are or have the potential to be unlimited community ambulators." Only a company that made something like computerized legs would think up a phrase like "community ambulator" to describe someone who wants to get up and walk around.

Our whole house is wireless—Ben's a computer nerd—so I took my laptop into his study to show him. His scripts have people getting blown up all the time, and I thought he might know about things like the C-Leg. He was clicking away at his keyboard, but he turned around and smiled when I came in. He's been acting strange ever since he and Mom had the fight about picking me up, and I wonder if maybe he isn't as unconcerned about it all as he's been acting.

"So why do you want to know about this?" he asked, when I showed him the screen.

"Jesse says he might get one. I was just trying to picture what it would be like to have to walk around on something like that."

"Oh." Ben gave me a funny look. "How old is Jesse?"

"I don't know. I think he's nineteen maybe. Too young to have to wear something like that." I jabbed a finger at the screen. I hadn't thought much about the war really until lately, but now the whole idea of it was making me furious.

"Are you upset about war or about Jesse?"

I wasn't really sure. About people getting blown up, I suppose. That's real, and pieces of them really come off, not like in Ben's movies where it's rubber and fake blood. And there are little kids, like Michael and Sarah, getting blown up too. "It's just not right," I said. "Why do we have to do that to each other?"

Ben nodded. "Oh, Angelfish. It's pretty painful when you get a social conscience, isn't it?"

He couldn't tell me much about the C-Leg though. "Pretty much everything in movies is made up," he said. "If the technology we need doesn't actually exist, we just lie."

———————

After dinner, Mom called me up. "Angie, honey…" I could tell she was using her working-up-to-something-in-a-casual-fashion voice. "Did you have fun last night? Trick-or-treating?"

"Yeah. And I'm not eating a bunch of candy."

"Darling, I was not calling you to quiz you on your candy consumption."

"Jesse's little brother and sister got all the candy. Well, maybe I stole a Heath bar, but that's all."

"Jesse. Mmmm. How old is Jesse Francis?"

"Mom, Ben asked me that. And you already know, anyway."

"Well, I … do you think maybe he's a little old?"

"For what?"

"Well, don't you think maybe he ought to be dating— girls his age?"

"There aren't any still in school. Mom, he needs a friend."

"Honey, you want to come have a coffee with me? Maybe we could talk."

I hate having "discussions" over the telephone, so I said okay and met her at the coffee bar downtown. We got cappuccinos and sat down at a corner table. Mom poked the froth in hers around with her spoon.

"Four years is a big age gap when you're fifteen," she said. "Later, it won't make much difference, but right now the difference is huge."

"Boys my age are idiots," I muttered.

"Granted. But still." Mom sighed. "I never thought I'd see the day when I'd encourage you to go out with Noah Michalski, but at least he's your age."

"Mom! He tried to stick his hand up my blouse and then he told everyone I let him do it!"

"I know. His mother says he's sorry."

"You've been talking to his *mother* about me?"

"Just in passing!" Mom looked guilty. And obviously she was scraping the bottom of the barrel if she was trying to fix me up with Noah.

"This is ridiculous. You never worried about my friends before."

"Jesse may be a more complicated friend than you think," Mom said.

I thought about the mazes he draws around the pictures in his books and on the backs of his binders. But am I supposed to just abandon him because he's four years older and he makes my mom nervous?

"An experience like war affects people," Mom continued. "There are things you just don't see, but they're there.

It affects things like perception … judgment. I don't know how stable Jesse is."

"He's perfectly stable!" I said.

"I'm just not comfortable having you go out with him," Mom said.

"I'm not 'going out' with him."

"How do you know how he feels about you?"

"He thinks I don't treat him like a freak, and he knows I don't gossip about him."

"He's too old for you."

"I'm not dating him."

We sat there and stared at each other. "Ben called you, didn't he?" I asked her.

"He thought I might be concerned."

And she paid attention to Ben this time instead of automatically taking the other side. That might be a good sign. But I didn't say that. "I tell you what," I offered. "I won't stop being friends with Jesse, but I promise that if anything at all gets weird, I'll tell you. Okay?" I left the definition of "weird" open.

Mom hesitated, then slurped down a mouthful of cappuccino. "That seems reasonable. *His* mother's worried, too."

"About me? She was nice when we were over there last night. And will you please stop discussing me with everybody's *mother*?"

"I'm not. It wasn't about you. She's worried about Jesse hanging around with younger kids and not people his own age."

"Then why did she send him back to school? And give him some time. Nobody his own age has a clue where he's been."

"And you do?"

"No, but I don't have to. I'm *not* his girlfriend."

"Okay," Mom said. "As long as you keep it that way."

I wondered then just how Mom happened to get married at sixteen. I also sat up straighter and quit poking my finger into the foam on my cappuccino and licking it, like I was someone who was actually mature enough to be friends with somebody older.

6

I was so encouraged by Mom actually listening to Ben,
even if it was about butting into my life, that I went over
to St. Thomas's on the way home from the coffee shop,
thinking that maybe Felix could convince Mom to come
back to Ben's, now that we know what Ben did to make her
so mad. People always listen to total strangers when they
won't listen to their families, who have already told them
the same thing.

And if Felix was in a war, like Mom thinks, maybe he
could tell her that Jesse isn't a dangerous nut. Although
Felix probably isn't the best example for that.

He was in the basement. I smelled ramen noodles cooking as soon as I started down the stairs. Wuffie was right—
Father Weatherford must know he's living here.

"Hey, Ange." He smiled up at me. He was sitting in a pile of clothes and sleeping bag on the floor, poking at a rickety saucepan on the hot plate. At least he hadn't put the noodles on the hot plate still in their foam cup. "I thought you might not come back."

"I thought I might not, too," I admitted.

"So what brings you our way? Intercession? Offerings? We have a special on indulgences this week."

In the Middle Ages, the church used to sell indulgences that cancelled out any sins you might have committed. Sometimes you could even buy them ahead of time. Now that was an idea. But I said, "Intercession. I want you to talk to Mom. I found out why she's mad at Ben and I want you to tell her to get over it."

"That's tactful," he said.

"Well, don't put it like that when you talk to her."

"And why is she mad?"

I told him, and he said, "I don't blame her."

"You don't understand. All writers use real stuff. She knows that—she does it herself. She described my naked butt in a poem once. I was two, but still."

"How many people saw the poem?"

"Probably not many. It was in some literary magazine. But when I was in middle school, some moron got hold of it and read it aloud in homeroom."

Felix smiled.

"It wasn't funny."

"No, but you should be able to sympathize with your mom."

"She should be able to sympathize with me."

"She's not trying to divorce *you*," he pointed out. He stirred the noodles and I was suddenly suspicious again.

"Are you putting the moves on my mom? Are you the last person I should be asking for help here?"

"I dunno, Ange. Maybe. I like your mom."

"Oh, shit." I sat down on the bottom stair. "You're too old for her. And you live in a basement," I told him. "She's not going to marry someone who lives in a basement."

"That's okay, I'm not ready for marriage." He started eating the noodles out of the pot with the wooden spoon.

"And you also claim you're St. Felix. You probably aren't even real."

"You think?" He stopped eating and looked as if he was considering that.

"You're a monk, aren't you? You can't go chasing women."

"I'm thinking of leaving the order."

I was getting exasperated. I hadn't seen Felix in a while and I'd forgotten what he was like. I was just trying to rattle him and he was taking it all literally. Talking to him was like talking to one of those toys that's programmed with certain sentences. They don't make sense, but sometimes they're weirdly appropriate. I wondered what Ben would make of him, and if I ought to tell Ben that Mom was seeing someone else and that the someone else was probably crazy. For the life of me, I couldn't make myself believe that Felix was dangerous.

"Okay, don't talk to Mom about Ben," I said. "But can

you tell her not to worry about me being friends with Jesse Francis?"

"Why is she worried?"

"She thinks he's too old for me, and that maybe he's not stable. But he needs somebody to be friends with."

"Yeah. I expect he does," Felix said.

"So will you talk to her?"

"Maybe she's right."

"That's so unfair!" I glared at him.

"Ange, there's more stuff in this universe than you know about. Jesse Francis has probably met some of it."

"Like you did?"

He was quiet after that, not eating, just looking across the room as if there were something there, which there wasn't.

"What does everybody think Jesse's going to *do*?" I demanded. "Turn into a werewolf when the moon gets full?"

"Even the man who is pure at heart and says his prayers at night," Felix said. "Prayers won't keep some things off you."

"Like what?" I insisted.

He shook his head and started eating again.

"*What?*"

"Stuff that gets in your dreams."

He'd closed up, and I could tell he wasn't going to say anything else. So I went home and took the Todal for a walk, which is what I do when I want to think. The Todal snuffled along, sucking up all the things only dogs can smell, while I thought about Mom and Ben and what on earth I could do about it. Everything I thought of sounded like a bad plot device.

What makes love last? How can you be in love with someone, and then not? And if you still are, how can you be mad enough to leave them? Mom is always restless, but this is out there even for her. What does she *want*? What do I want, for that matter? If I find someone to be in love with and marry, and he actually loves me back, what kind of guarantee do I have that it will all work out? That I won't end up divorced with six children, living on food stamps? I worried that one around in my head till bedtime, but I didn't get anywhere with it.

In the middle of the night I was in the jungle somewhere. The air was steaming hot. It was like trying to breathe in a sauna, but it stank. It smelled like a backed-up sewer, overlaid with gasoline. Light kept dropping out of the darkness over the tree line in sharp flashes, freezing everything like a photograph for a few seconds, and each time I could see a man lying just beyond the hole I was crouched in, his eyes stuck open and his feet hanging over the edge. Another explosion shook everything and I woke up in a sweat.

I just sat there for a minute, shaking. I don't usually have nightmares, and this one was horrible and *nothing* like any bad dream I've ever had before. Usually I dream the brakes on my bike don't work and I'm flying down a hill into a tree, or there's the one where I turn on the lights in the house at night and none of them come on. Nothing like this. I looked at the clock. It was two a.m. My heart was still thumping. I took deep yoga breaths, like Mom does, until it settled down again. I lay down and punched the pillow into a better shape and didn't wake up again or dream anything else.

"You look awful," Lily said the next morning.

"I was up late." I didn't say anything about the dream.

The dream came back the next night, though, and this time it scared me to death. It was like being in an awful movie, absolutely real and utterly terrifying, because I was somebody *else*. I was back in the jungle, lying in the shadows along a canal. We were waiting for something.

"How can you tell VC from civilians?" a voice asked out of the darkness, and another voice said, "If it's out there, you shoot it. Anything out at night is VC."

Mosquitoes were whining in the grass around my head like tiny power tools almost out of human hearing range. A fish jumped in the water. I could see its silvery flip and the ripples spreading out on the black water. Five boats came through the mist on the canal with a faint plop of oars.

Then the night exploded in gunfire, all lit up by red arcs over the canal and the fire of a burning boat. Men in black pajamas were scrambling across the decks of other boats, firing bullets through the trees. Their shadows danced on the bank like huge monsters. Then their boats went up in a roar of orange flame.

"We got swimmers, Sarge!" Someone on the bank fired into the canal. A face floated up below me, just black eyes and a wide mouth, hands clawing at the grass. Another shot blasted him into a red lump that sank down through the water again. On the river, one last man was hanging onto his burning boat. He lifted his gun and fired before he went up in flames too. Farther down the bank someone slid through the mud into the water, his arms flailing.

"Doc!"

I heaved myself up, running low. Someone else dragged the boy out of the water before he drowned. There was a hole in his chest the size of a hand and he was spitting blood along with water. I could hear air bubbling in the wound. His eyes stared at me, horrified. In the dream, I knew what to do. I slapped a pad of gauze and Vaseline on the wound to try to seal it and injected him with a morphine syringe.

"Dust-off!"

The medevac chopper came down over the trees, lit up by the burning boats on the water. As it lifted off, another sound wailed through the thick air above it, over the chopper's rotors, hideous and otherworldly: the sound of a baby crying, distorted by volume and the tree cover. The soundship hovered over the river and then banked, heading upstream. A message followed the wailing in shrill Vietnamese: "Friendly baby, GVN baby, don't let this happen to *your* baby! Resist the Viet Cong today!"

I sat up in bed, tangled in the sheets, with that godawful baby ringing in my ears. I had known what the loudspeaker was saying. How did I know that?

It was two a.m. again. I was afraid to go to sleep. The only time I drifted off, I dreamed I was sewing up a goat. The goat was anesthetized, on a table, and I was pulling bullets out of it and sewing it up. In my dream, it opened its yellow eyes and looked right at me with those strange sideways pupils, and I woke up in a sweat. After that I got up and turned on all the lights in my room and read *A Tale of Two Cities*, which was our English assignment and certainly didn't help much.

The dreams stayed in my head all day, but I'd figured out where they came from. As soon as school was out, I went over to the church. Felix was upstairs this time, polishing windows.

"What do you think you're doing?"

"Cleaning the Virgin here," he said. He rubbed her face gently with his rag. The baby in her arms beamed out at us. Friendly baby.

"Get out of my head!"

He looked puzzled. "What are you talking about?"

"I mean the nightmares! And don't tell me you don't know anything about it. They're coming out of *your* head!" I was so mad I didn't even stop to think about the fact that that was sort of impossible.

"I get nightmares all the time," Felix said quietly. "That's not news."

"Well, you're giving them to me!" I told him. "*I'm* having your dreams."

"You're kidding."

"On a riverbank? Boats on fire? There's a big helicopter broadcasting in a foreign language and I *understand* it?"

"Ah, shit." He looked white.

"Sewing up goats? What is that about sewing up goats?"

"Oh, man." He dropped the rag on a pew and sat down.

"You were in Vietnam, weren't you? That's what I'm dreaming about, isn't it?"

"They trained us on goats. They shot them with M-16s and then we practiced sewing them up again."

"That's awful!"

"Yeah. You quit feeling sorry for the goats, though, after you scoop up some boy's guts and tape them to his chest because you can't stuff them back in since someone's stepped on them and they're contaminated."

My stomach heaved. "I'm not going to dream about that, am I?"

"I don't know. I don't know why you're having my dreams at all, but I guess you are. I'm sorry."

"You didn't do it on purpose? Because I was asking you questions?"

"No! Christ, no!" He looked so horrified I felt sorry for him. They were pretty awful dreams; I couldn't think what it would be like to have them all the time. "You were a medic?" I asked.

"Yeah. I was in pre-med when my lottery number came up."

"Lottery?" Who would want to win a prize like that?

"There were so many protests about rich kids getting draft deferments for being in college and poor kids going to Nam that the government started a lottery. They drew birthdates, and the guys with the first birthdate drawn, they went first."

"What did your family do?"

"My mom wanted me to go to Canada, but my old man said no way. He put me on a bus for the induction center."

I thought about Jesse's mom and the way she'd looked at his father. "What was it like?" I asked.

"Trust me, you don't want to know."

"I didn't want to dream about it, either. Did you do this to me to scare me away from Jesse?"

"I told you, I didn't do it. I wouldn't do that."

"Well, something did it. Somebody did it."

"God moves in mysterious ways," Felix said.

"You think God is giving me your dreams?"

"Well, he cancelled my sainthood. If he can do that, he can do what he wants to. Maybe I'll get your dreams."

"*No!*" I said. I did not want him poking around in my dreams. Dreams are too personal. Not to mention embarrassing. I've had dreams I wouldn't even tell Lily about.

"No, I probably won't," he agreed. "I'd like to be fifteen again, though. I'd like to have those dreams back."

"If you're St. Felix of Valois, you were studying in an abbey when you were fifteen," I pointed out.

"We dream anyway," he said.

"What happened after you got drafted?"

"Goats." He didn't seem to have any trouble shifting back and forth between lives. "Boys. Boys with their feet blown off. They took 'em away so fast in the dust-off chopper, I never knew whether they lived or not. Except for sometimes. Sometimes if they died they came back and saw me."

"Ghosts?" I had a horrible vision of a soldier with his guts taped to his chest, leaning over Felix's bed. No wonder he was crazy.

"Yeah. There're two or three I see pretty regularly. Kid with a sucking chest wound—the one you dreamed about."

"I don't want to dream about that again," I said. Something occurred to me. "Are you a doctor now? Did you finish med school when you came home?"

He shook his head, staring down at the pew. It was old, dark wood, shiny with two hundred years of people's butts. "I lost my taste for it. I thought I could save the world, you know, and I couldn't even save some kid who stepped on a booby trap."

"What did you do?"

"This and that. I worked construction some. Cut trail. Planted trees. I stayed home till my old man got tired of me."

"Felix? What am I going to do about the dreams?" I was dead tired from not getting any sleep, and totally scared of them coming back.

"I don't know," he said. "Pray?"

7

It was Friday night and Grandma Alice had lit the candles and said the Sabbath prayers, so I thought maybe that would do. But I still thought about the dreams all the way through dinner, scared to death I was going to have them again. Finally, Grandma Alice patted my hand and said, "Angie? Honey? You look like you don't feel so good."

"I don't."

"In the stomach? Or up here?" She pointed at her forehead.

"It's kind of hard to tell," I said. "I've been having bad dreams."

"What about, kiddo?" Ben looked worried too, now.

"About war, sort of." I didn't say which war. I didn't want them to think I was as crazy as Felix. "And it's not because I've been hanging out with Jesse," I added before Ben could open his mouth.

"No, wars just do that," Grandma Alice said. "They get in the air. I remember when Ben's father was overseas, during the war."

I knew she meant World War II.

"I was a hostess at the Hollywood Canteen," she continued. Grandma Alice's father ran a movie studio; she was a Hollywood princess when she was young. "We'd serve coffee and dance with the boys who were home on leave. It made me feel like I was doing something to help keep my husband safe. Some kind of sympathetic magic—I danced with those lonesome boys here, and somebody would be nice to him over there."

"Did you dream about the stuff they told you?"

"They never talked about the war, really. They just wanted to be normal for a few days. But yes, I dreamed. My head made things up. All David's letters home to me were censored, of course. They weren't allowed to write about troop movements or anything that might give the enemy information. So we pretended we were discussing movie plots when he wanted to tell me where they were shipping him."

"You never told me any of this, Mom," Ben said.

"Well, it didn't come up," Grandma Alice said lightly. "I was just glad when your brothers got through Vietnam without getting drafted. You, I didn't have to worry about; you were too young."

"Now we have nice new wars." Ben sighed and speared a lamb chop.

"There was another demonstration downtown," I said. I'd passed it on the way home from St. Thomas's. "There were a lot of people holding candles and signs, and they were selling bumper stickers that said WHEN JESUS SAID LOVE YOUR ENEMIES, I THINK HE MEANT DON'T KILL THEM."

Ben smiled. "Your mom wanted me to go stand with them. *She* can't, because the school board will get on her case, so she wanted me to take a stand for the family's political convictions. I mentioned that she seemed to have forgotten she's left me."

That almost made me laugh, it sounded so like Mom. When I got ready for bed I thought about what Felix had said, about praying. *Please God,* I thought, *just let me have my own dreams.* I don't know whether God really listens to individual people or not. If he does, he must have a thousand ears. And I would think the people getting blown up in Afghanistan and murdered in Africa would drown out people like me. Just in case he *was* listening, though, I said, *Please make Mom come home. Please get her back together with Ben.*

How can he keep things straight, all the things people are asking him? What does he do when two people ask for opposite things? And what about all the people who keep saying God is on their side? How can he be on both sides? And how could he be on anybody's side who wants to blow somebody else up in his name?

Even the churches can't decide that one. There's a big sign outside the Baptist church that says SUPPORT OUR

Troops and one outside the Unitarian church that says Peace Vigil 7 p.m.

At the peace demonstration there was a car with a bumper sticker that said:

Dyslexics, remember that Dog loves you.
A message from the untied church of Dog.

Maybe God really is a dog, and he loves everybody but he can't help them do things or get things or win the lottery, or wars. That probably isn't an idea I should talk over with Father Weatherford. With Wuffie or Grandma Alice, maybe. Sometimes I think those two old ladies know stuff nobody else does. Grandma Alice had a cousin who died in the Holocaust. The family tried to get her out but it was too late. Grandma Alice doesn't talk about it much. If *she* still believes in God, I guess he must be out there somewhere.

I went to sleep thinking about God, and Felix's dreams stayed out of my head. But in the morning they were still so real in my memory—as if they had to be real somewhere, and inhabit somebody's head—that I hoped that didn't mean Felix was having them. It was Saturday, and the more I thought about it, the more I worried about him. So I went back over to St. Thomas's and found him in the herb garden at the back of the church, weeding.

The herb garden was the Altar Society's idea—to make the church look just like it did when it was founded in 1800-something. Back then, the Indians they were trying to convert would have been the ones working in the garden; not really voluntarily, but the Altar Society has sort of sidestepped that fact. The Church was really awful to the Indians, it's a wonder any of the Chumash people around here will even speak to us.

Felix had on that ratty old bathrobe, and he was kneeling in a pool of sun by a stone bench, setting out lavender starts. He was barefoot and the bald spot in his gray hair looked like a monk's tonsure. He really did look like he might be a brother in some old monastery.

"Hey," I said.

He sat up on his heels and smiled at me. "Hey, yourself."

"If I don't have those dreams, does it mean you get them?" I asked him. They were so awful. Maybe I could stand them for a while, just to keep him from having them. After all, he'd been taking on my troubles since I was nine.

"Did you get them again last night?" He looked worried now.

"No," I said. "Did you?"

"No, I dreamed I was riding a camel through this big mountain of whipped cream."

I couldn't tell whether he was lying to make me feel better or not. It sounded like a dream somebody might have.

"Fish were swimming out of my ears," he added.

I had to laugh. And I could tell he wasn't going to tell me whether it was true or not.

"Did you pray?" he asked me.

"Kind of. I thought about God, and how everybody

says he's on their side. He can't be on both sides." Unless, of course, he *is* a dog. Dogs love everybody.

"That's why every religion claims that everyone else's God is really the devil," Felix said.

"Why can't they all be the same God with different names?"

"Watch out. That's the kind of thinking that got me un-sainted."

"How do you know?" I asked him. "You said you didn't know why it happened." Now I was talking like he really was St. Felix.

"Well, being St. Felix is very specific to Christianity. I mean, the Virgin came and rang the cloister bells for me and all."

I suppose he read the same *Lives of the Saints* in the parish library that I did. At any rate, I wasn't going to get into a discussion with him about whether he'd actually seen the Virgin Mary.

But I must have looked skeptical, because he said, "If Juan Diego can see her, I can see her."

Juan Diego is the Aztec Indian who supposedly saw the Virgin of Guadalupe and converted all his friends afterward. He maybe didn't really exist any more than St. Felix of Valois did, although the Pope canonized him. But I couldn't help it; I said, "What was she like?"

Felix stared across the herb garden, like he was looking straight through the adobe wall, and said, "This woman had a baby, all wrapped in a shawl, you know?"

"The Virgin?"

"No, she shoved the baby at the lieutenant and he took it. Then she ran like a bat outta hell, and the baby exploded. The lieutenant was standing under this tree, you know, and there were scraps of him and the baby hanging off the tree. The tree was all burned black. That was when I saw her. She was just hanging in the air over the tree, in her blue gown, and she looked so sad."

"Oh my God." I sat down on the bench. There was no way I was going to remind him that he'd just said she rang the bells for him in the monastery. It was clear that this was where he'd *really* seen her. Or seen *something*.

"She had on this starry cloak," he said softly. "And she said, 'You're late.'"

"Felix—"

"Scared the shit outta me, because I didn't want to go, you know, not where the lieutenant had gone." He looked up at me and he was back in the herb garden again, not wherever he'd been a second before.

"Do you dream about that?" I asked him, scared to get an answer.

He smiled. "Just about the Virgin. She always has her hands full of roses, that's how I know it's her."

I hoped he was telling the truth. I did *not* want to have the dream about the baby. If I had to, I thought, bargaining with whoever was in charge of these things, I would take the one about the boy with his insides taped to his chest instead.

"Felix, is that what it was like for Jesse?" I asked. "In Afghanistan?"

"I don't know. Alike and different, I expect. There's a kid who was in Afghanistan in a group I go to sometimes."

"What kind of group? You mean, like, a support group?" I wondered if he tries to tell *them* he's St. Felix.

"Yeah. At the VA."

Maybe a support group would be good for Jesse, I thought. I hung around while Felix put the rest of the lavender starts in the bed, and on the way home I bought a Peace Now bumper sticker from the Unitarians, who were having another vigil. I asked Ben if I could put it on his car. He said he doubted a bumper sticker here would have much influence there, but go ahead, peace was a fine sentiment for the season, what with Thanksgiving coming up.

———

On Monday, a group of kids were selling the bumper stickers at school, so I bought another one and put it on my art portfolio. Jesse saw it as soon as I came into class and made a sort of snorting noise.

"What?" I said.

"Huge political statement," he said, trying to get comfortable on his stool with the artificial leg.

"That's what Ben said," I admitted. "But you have to do something. I can't go to demonstrations. I'm too young to drive."

"And you would want to ... why?" he asked.

That kind of surprised me. "Because something that

gives people permanent nightmares can't be something we ought to be doing," I said.

"Leave my fucking dreams out of this!" he snapped at me, glaring.

I sucked my breath in—he looked so mad all of a sudden. "I didn't mean *your* dreams," I said hastily. I didn't know he *had* dreams, although I expect he must. Anybody would. I wasn't sure I could explain what I did mean, but he looked too mad to listen to me anyway.

"No, of course not." Now he sounded sarcastic and mean. "I'm not the only headcase you know."

"Actually, you're not!"

"*Peace now*," he said in a whiny voice. "You have no clue what it's about, none, do you?"

"I know you got hurt," I said. I wasn't sure what else to say to him. It was like he'd suddenly turned into somebody totally different. His face was tight, and there was that tic beside his eye that looked as if something under his skin was trying to get out.

"You don't know shit!" He grabbed a black marker and scrawled it all over the bumper sticker on my portfolio.

"I know people have to take a side for what they believe in!" I pulled my portfolio away from him. I could feel myself tearing up and I bit down on my lip to try to stop it.

Jesse pounded his fist on the art table, rattling it. "No, I don't!" He was loud, and everyone swiveled around to stare at us. "It's none of your business! Or theirs! I'm not your goddamn anti-war poster boy! And tell the VFW to go to hell too! I'm not going to be their tame hero! Leave me alone! All of you, just leave me the fuck alone!" He was shouting now, so angry he was spitting his words in my face. "Leave me the fuck alone!" he yelled again, and kicked his stool away with his good leg. It slammed against the next table. His portfolio slid off our table onto the floor, all his sketches falling out of it.

Mr. Petrillo flew across the room. "Jesse!"

"You leave me alone, too!" Jesse shoved past him and lurched around the tables, stepping on his drawings. He yanked the classroom door open and slammed it against the wall so hard the windows rattled. He turned around and threw the marker back in the room before he left.

"Oh. My. God," a girl in the corner said. There were a couple of uncertain snickers from the other tables.

"That was scary."

"Jesus, Arnaz, you always have that effect on guys?" someone said to me.

Someone else laughed. My face was burning.

"Jesse has … issues, obviously," Mr. Petrillo said. He looked pretty shook up himself. "Let's just leave him to deal with them, and … I'll be back in a moment. Please work on your self-portraits while I'm gone."

I picked up Jesse's portfolio and collected the sketches that were scattered on the floor. A couple of them were torn or had footprints on them. There were a lot of them that were just mazes, in all different colors, harsh angular patterns that were really kind of pretty but sad at the same time. His self-portrait had mazes all around his head, too, stiff dark ones that blended with his hair. I slid them back in the portfolio and tied the top. I wondered what I should do with it and I wanted to cry.

The noise in the classroom slowly picked up again.

"That dude's just crazy."

"You think Petrillo's gone to get the cops?"

"Man, I would. That dude needs to be in the psych ward."

———

Lily, on the other hand, said it wasn't unusual when I told her about it. "PTSD. Post-traumatic stress disorder. It can manifest as rage." Her mom is a psychologist. "You get it from trauma. Not just from wars—anybody can get it. Rape victims, for instance. Or people who've been in floods, or anything really heavy."

"I guess that would be Jesse," I said. "I've still got his portfolio. Should I just give it to Mr. Petrillo, or should I take it to him? I really want to see if he's okay."

"Mmm." Lily bit her lip—channeling her mom, I think. "Take it to him, but not by yourself. And wait and see if he comes back to school first. If he doesn't, I'll go with you."

8

I thought about Jesse all this week, but he didn't come back to school. And then on Sunday, Father Weatherford came bustling up to the youth group after Mass with the worst idea I've ever heard.

"We're going to put our little church on the map this year, my friends." He beamed at us. "*We* are going to have a Las Posadas walk at Christmas, followed by a live nativity!"

We all looked at each other as if our collective doom had been announced. Noah Michalski pointed his finger down his throat behind Father Weatherford's back and made gagging faces.

Las Posadas means "the inns" in Spanish. It's a big procession where Mary and Joseph go around knocking on neighborhood doors and getting turned away, and finally, at the house that lets them in, there's a big party. Father Weatherford is going to make a pageant of it, and march us down Ayala Avenue to the church, where we'll end up with a live nativity and a cast of thousands.

"I have the cast all worked out," he said. "Angie, you're going to be our Mary. And..." He let his eye wander over the rest of us, then held up one finger as if he'd just thought of it. "And Noah, you will be our Joseph!"

This was clearly Father Weatherford's idea for bringing the stray lamb back to the fold, since Noah hardly ever comes to church. It was just his bad luck his mother dragged him along that morning.

I tried to think of how to say *I'd rather be crucified* in a way that wouldn't offend Father Weatherford, and I could tell that Noah was, too, but by then Father was doling out supporting roles as innkeepers and magi, and the usual cast of shepherds and angels. I have never seen anyone look so thrilled over a terrible idea. "I've made arrangements for live animals—sheep and camels and a donkey for Mary to ride!"

Noah honked in my ear and flapped his hands over his head like donkey ears.

"Shut *up*!" I stomped on his foot.

So, I'm going to ride a donkey down Ayala Avenue while Noah leads it. It'll probably buck me off. We'll stop at any store that Father Weatherford can get to go along with it all, and end up at the nativity set in front of the church, where the sheep and camels will be waiting by the manger. I will produce a baby doll previously hidden under the straw in the manger (at least he doesn't want it to be produced from under my dress), and the Baby Jesus will be born. I'm not even going to report on the stupid suggestions Noah made about all this.

I was so disgusted, I told Wuffie I would walk home. I went around to the back garden and told Felix about it.

"I'll die if I have to be in a pageant with that idiot and have a baby." I sat down on a bench beside where Felix was weeding. The air smelled like sage. "Nobody can talk about anything but sex, but Noah Michalski is the worst. He laughed all the way through Biology while Ms. Knight was explaining how trees pollinate. And my mom would rather I went out with him than Jesse!"

It felt like it did when I used to talk to Felix's statue, which was weird. But he already knew the backstory, as Ben would say.

"Ah, he'll grow up," Felix said now. "He may not even be a bad kid. You might marry him some day."

I looked horrified.

"Just don't get in the back seat of a car with him now."

"I wouldn't get in the same room with him if I could help it."

"How's Jesse?"

"Did Mom tell you to ask me that?" I was immediately suspicious.

"Nah. So how is he?"

"He blew up in art class. He started shouting at me and he threw things."

"Mm." Felix ran his hands through the thyme, kind of fluffing it and thinking.

"Lily says he has post-traumatic stress disorder."

"You bet he does. And how does Lily know so much?"

"Her mom's a psychologist."

"Mm," he said again.

"So what do I do now?"

"Take it easy. Give him space. Does he see a shrink?"

"I think so. He said something about it."

Felix nodded. "That's usually good. You get prime nightmares being zipped up in a body bag while you're still alive, I bet."

"They do that?"

"Standard procedure now. They found out they can keep 'em alive longer if they don't lose body heat. They call 'em 'hot pockets,' but they're body bags and everyone knows it. Like taking a nap in your own coffin. If you don't make it, they just zip it up the rest of the way."

"That's horrible!"

"Medically speaking, it's a good procedure. It's a shame we didn't think of it in Nam."

"How do you know about it?"

"I pay attention. You want to know what happens after they're taken off the battlefield?"

"Are you okay to talk about it?" I asked.

"Yeah. I was never around for that part of it. Half the time I didn't know whether the guys I sent on made it or not. Sometimes you'd hear on the radio." He started to stare off into the distance again, and then he snapped his head around and looked at me, eyebrows raised.

"Yeah. I do want to know." I thought I did. I was pretty sure I did.

"So, once the medevac chopper picks one up, they'll take him to the hospital in Kandahar. Or her, these days. They'll do CPR on the way if there isn't any pulse. No flight medic wants a kid to die in his chopper. One guy told me that if they die in your chopper, they hang around."

"Hang around?"

"Yeah. And a chopper isn't very big."

I thought about being haunted by soldiers you'd tried to save. Like Felix's dreams, only while you're awake.

"The ones that make it, they'll fly them to Germany, and maybe their folks will come over. But they won't remember it, not if they're badly hurt. They dope 'em up pretty well. Lots of them don't really wake up till they're at Walter Reed in Washington. Then they find out what's missing."

I tried to imagine waking up one morning and discovering I had no left leg. Jesse's parents flew out to Germany, and then back to Washington with him. Mom told me. His mom stayed there in Washington until he came home.

"When they send them home," Felix said, "there's rehab, and sometimes they have to go back in. There's a complication that happens to amputees. The bone that's left grows all over, into the rest of their leg, into the places where the flesh got damaged. It's supposed to be rare, but it happens to battle amputees all the time."

That sounded almost creepier than anything else.

"Your friend dodged that one, it looks like."

"So how do I talk to him now?"

Felix chuckled. "Carefully?"

"I thought I was. I mean, I have no idea why he blew up. It made me feel awful."

"What started it?"

"I had a stop-the-war sticker on my binder. He said I was clueless. And the VFW was clueless."

"Oh. Well, most of us know that one. If you say the war's all wrong, you're saying your buds died for nothing. If you say it's all cool, you have to not notice a lot."

"That would be hard. But I get to have opinions, don't I?" I felt kind of resentful. I know I've had it easy, and Jesse went through stuff I can't even imagine, but I don't take well to being told to suppress my opinions.

"Sure," Felix said. He ruffled my hair, just a kindly old saint in his fake Mission garden. "It wasn't about you, kiddo, not really."

———

I tried to keep that in mind when Lily and I went to take Jesse's art portfolio back in the afternoon. Since he hadn't been to school for a week, I was afraid he wasn't coming back. I really missed him, and I had this awful image of him in his bedroom, drawing mazes on the walls.

His mother opened the door when we rang the bell.

"Uh. We have Jesse's art portfolio," I said when she didn't say anything. "We thought maybe he'd want it."

She looked hopeful at that, like she really, really hoped he would. "Come in, girls." She left us in the living room and we heard her feet pattering down the hall and a tap on his door. We couldn't hear what he said, but after a minute he came out, kind of blinking like he'd been in a cave. He was wearing shorts, and I could tell Lily was trying not to look at the leg. His hair looked like he hadn't combed it, and his shirt like he'd slept in it. I bet he had.

"Hi!" I said brightly, feeling like Miss Congeniality. I held out the portfolio.

"Oh." Jesse looked at it for a few seconds as if it might not be his. Then he took it and he smiled at me. "Thank you."

"We, uh, thought you might want it."

"Yeah. Have I missed much?" Now he was sounding like somebody who has just been out with a cold.

"Uh. Not much. We're supposed to finish our self-portraits."

"Portrait of the artist as a young headcase."

Jesse's mother looked like she was about to cry.

"You could do that. Sure," I said, because I was getting annoyed with him. I'll never make a good nurse.

Then he smiled at me again. He really has the sweetest smile. "I'm sorry I was an asshole. I'll turn it in on Monday."

———

Jesse's self-portrait was a face surrounded by mazes—no big surprise—but at least he actually showed up at school. If it had been any of the rest of us, Mr. Petrillo would have got on our cases for being trite and self-indulgent, but he didn't say anything like that to Jesse. Everybody is extremely nervous about Jesse right now. But Jesse just smiled at me and flicked my hair after Mr. Petrillo went to look at other people's portraits.

"Hey, Duchess. Thanks for dragging me out of my cave. It means a lot to me that you'd do that." He sort of patted my head and tugged on a curl.

"Sure."

"Can I buy you a coffee after school? I have something for you."

I wondered what it was all afternoon, until after class we walked down to the coffee bar and Jesse pulled a folder out of his bookbag. There was a picture of the Duchess of Alba inside, a big print on nice paper. It wasn't the one I'd seen online, but I recognized her right away.

The barista called his name and he set two cups down on the table while I looked at the picture. I could tell Jesse was watching me to see what I thought.

In this one, the Duchess has on a white dress and a red sash and a red bow in her hair. Her little white dog has a red bow too. Her black hair is even wilder than in the other picture, curly and all over the place. She's not exactly pretty, but I wouldn't mind anybody thinking I look like her. I've taped her up on my wall.

"This one is known as the White Duchess," Jesse explained. "Goya painted her a lot. She was his mistress, I think."

"Aha. Backstory." I laughed. "Thank you." I set it with my bookbag, away from the coffee.

"My little sister said she looks like a fairy duchess and wanted to draw wings on her. She thought you'd like that. She's pretty much convinced that everybody's improved by wings."

I said, "I wanted to be a horse when I was that age."

"You make a better girl." Jesse smiled at me.

"So what did you play when you were little?" I asked him. "Batman, like your brother?"

His mouth kind of tightened for a second. "G.I. Joe."

Oops.

Then he brushed my hand. "It's okay. I'm not going to go off on you. I feel really bad about that. I've been afraid you wouldn't like me anymore."

I shook my head. Maybe after what he's been through, he's earned the right to go off on people once in a while. "I was probably clueless," I said.

"No, you're the smartest person I've met in a long time. Just being with you makes me calm down. That's what my shrink says I need—to be around someone who takes me as I am, and then I won't feel like I need to be that way so much."

I drank my cappuccino and did not poke my finger in the foam. "I'm trying to untangle that," I said, but I knew what he meant.

"You make me feel calm," Jesse said. "I'll think about you when all the rug rats are shrieking and shooting off ray guns at Thanksgiving and I want to dive under the table."

"Family fun." I thought about my own family, which has no little kids, just two adults acting like it, and we both laughed. I like Jesse a lot.

And his talking about Thanksgiving gave me an absolutely brilliant idea, which I started work on the minute I got home. Thanksgiving is next week, and if there is any time that Mom is a sucker for family and sentiment, it's Thanksgiving. She has this weird Norman Rockwell picture of a big family gathered around the turkey, saying grace and being grateful to each other. She also has a habit of bringing home French teachers whose wives have just left them, and church ladies who have lost most of their marbles and are liable to set things on fire if they cook turkey.

"Absolutely not!" she said when I made my pitch.

I tucked the phone under my ear and practiced looking sincere in the mirror. "Mom, it's Thanksgiving. I can't stand the idea of having to pick one of you to have Thanksgiving with." I let my voice quaver a bit, which wasn't hard, because I really was about to cry. I miss Mom like anything, even if I won't tell her that.

"Oh, Angie." I could hear her sniffle. "I just don't think it's a good idea for me to come to Ben's..."

"You don't have to," I said. "We'll come to Wuffie's. I've already asked Ben and Grandma Alice. There's more room there for a big dinner, anyway." In the past we've always gone to Wuffie's; Mom has never actually cooked the turkey herself (except for the year I was six and we lived in Venice—California, not Italy—and the guy she was seeing sliced his thumb carving it and we all went to the emergency room).

"It'll be good for Grandma Alice to have some company," I added. Mom likes Grandma Alice. "And Wuffie and Grandpa Joe will like to see us. And maybe we could ask Felix—I bet he doesn't have anyplace else to go. It'll be easier for you and Ben if there's someone else there, I bet." That was my secret ploy. Mom likes to do the gathering-in-the-unfortunate thing, and Ben will get a heads-up just in case Felix really is competition. I could hear Mom thinking about it.

"Well..."

"Good!" I said. "I'll tell Ben. We'll be there at four."

I ran over to St. Thomas's and invited Felix before Mom could call back and change her mind. He looked startled, and so did Ben when I told him we would be picking up a homeless guy to take him to Wuffie's, but I just rolled right over both of them. It's all set.

———

And Jesse is doing the sweetest thing. The morning after he bought me coffee and gave me the print of the White Duchess, I opened my locker and this little drawing fluttered out. He must have slipped it in through the vent slots. Noah was standing right there (he has the locker next to mine, another trial in my life), so I took it into the girls' bathroom to look at it. It isn't signed, but I know it's from Jesse—it's a drawing of a horse with a huge, curly black mane and tail that's bigger than she is (it's clearly a girl horse). And she has wings, but they're drawn to look like they're stuck on with duct tape and there's a little sign hanging from one of them, like the tags on pillows, that says, WINGS ADDED BY ORDER OF THE PRINCESS. REGULATION 252, UNIVERSAL WINGS ACCESS BILL. I've taped it up on my bedroom wall next to the picture of the White Duchess.

And the next morning there was another one, this time a picture of a G.I. Joe doll and a plastic horse figurine sitting on a shelf. They're looking at each other. And now there's a drawing in my locker every morning. He never says anything about them when I see him in art class. I don't say anything, either. It's like a secret code, or getting an anonymous Valentine, only I know who it's from.

This Sunday we had a Posadas rehearsal after Mass. Father Weatherford handed us our lines, which consist of: "I beg a room of you, for my wife is great with child," on Noah's part, and "I am blessed among women" and "What, no room at all?" on mine. The shepherds stood around baaing at each other, pretending to be sheep.

"We need a room 'cause my wife's great in the sack," Noah said, and everybody thought that was hysterical. Father Weatherford spoke severely to him about respect.

"Behold, I bring you tidings of great joy," Mary Mahan informed me.

We'd all brought our work clothes, as instructed, and after we'd trooped off to the bathrooms to change into them, Father Weatherford handed out saws and hammers, which I could have told him was a mistake. He took them back again when the Wise Men started fencing. He finally got everybody settled down somehow (I wouldn't take that man's job—not that the church would let me, being still backward about women priests), and Noah and I got the assignment to make a manger out of an orange crate. Not only are we the happy parents, we get to furnish the nursery.

Noah held the two crosspieces for the legs against the end of the crate, which said FILLMORE LEMON ASSOCIA-TION on it. "Can you hold it steady while I hammer?" he asked me through a mouthful of nails.

I held it while he did his studly guy-in-a-toolbelt thing. "I guess it could be worse," he said, through the nails. "We could have to be the sheep."

"I'm surprised you said you'd be in it at all," I told him. "You hardly ever come to Mass."

"I'm scoring points with my mom. She'll let me drive the car when I get my license if I promise to consider my relationship with God and don't get in any more trouble at school."

"Good luck on that."

"Hey. That wasn't my fault."

He flipped the crate over and I held the other end while he hammered the legs on in a manly fashion. I hoped he would miss my thumb.

The shepherds were putting up the stable walls. The

pageant's still a month away but since it never rains here, Father Weatherford thinks it will be good advertisement for the event if we put the stable up and hang a sign and lights from it. He was trying to untangle some Christmas lights while Missy Escobar painted angels on the sign.

Noah set the manger upright and wiggled it. It didn't rock too much. Then he actually asked me if I wanted to go down to the Frosty Freeze, and I was so surprised I said yes.

We walked there, and then had to dodge a clump of sticky little kids and a couple of Ayala High seniors making out at one of the tables. Noah got us each a Mister Softee ice cream with chocolate dip and actually paid for both of them himself.

"Uh, I've been sort of wanting to talk to you," he said as I nipped the crunchy chocolate top off. Once you break it, it always starts to slide, and I chased a flake down the side of the cone.

"I mean, I sort of heard you're still mad at me," he went on, when I didn't say anything.

"No shit." If he was going to apologize for the incident with my shirt, I thought I'd make him really get into it. Even if his mother was making him do it.

"So, it wasn't like I was trying to trash you or anything."

"Of course not. If you'd wanted to do that, you'd have told the world that I let you feel me up."

"I guess I wanted to think you had." He gave me a kind of goofy smile.

"Do you have any idea how embarrassing that was?"

"No, I guess not." He looked penitent, and I thought it was probably the best I was going to get. He really didn't have any idea.

We finished our cones and walked back to St. Thomas's. Missy's sign was propped up against the stable waiting for Felix to hang it. Her angels looked really good, with trumpets and everything announcing the coming attraction.

I was surprised to see Jesse leaning up against the stable next to the sign, looking antsy and worried. "Where have you been?" he said as soon as he saw me.

"What do you mean?"

"I came to give you a ride home after rehearsal. And make sure you were all right." He shot Noah a look.

"I only live two blocks away. But that was really nice of you," I said in a hurry, because Noah was giving Jesse a look back. I'd told Jesse about the pageant, of course, and how I'd rather be dead in a ditch than be in it. I may have overdramatized a bit to make him feel sorry for me.

Then Noah said, "Hey, Van Gogh. Stick to the love letters in the locker, okay?"

Jesse's face flamed up bright red at that. He unfolded himself from under Missy's sign and lurched over to Noah. "Listen up, you little shit..."

And that was when Felix came around the corner of the church with a hammer and nails. He gave me and Noah his own look right away and said, "Hey, troops, I'm about to clean those bathrooms. You want to get your clothes out of there for me?" Then he said to Jesse, "Give me a hand with these angels, will you?"

Noah had enough sense to keep quiet until we were inside. "Asshole," he muttered as soon as we were out of earshot. "That dude's a psycho, man. Pictures in your locker—that's creepy. You ought to look out for him."

"You shut up!" I snapped. "It's none of your business!"

"I'm just saying…"

"Well, don't! Because you don't know anything!" I slammed the girls' bathroom door behind me. Or tried to—it has one of those things that makes it creep closed.

When I came out, Noah was gone and Jesse was sitting on a hay bale in the stable talking to Felix. I was glad; talking to Felix might be good for Jesse. I stuck my head in and said, "Thanks for the offer, but I'd better walk home. I promised Grandma Alice I'd help clean the house."

Jesse said, "I'll see you at school then." He looked better, like talking to Felix had settled him down.

And if Noah says one single thing about Jesse, or about those drawings, I'll kill him.

9

So naturally I called Lily as soon as I got home. "What is *wrong* with boys? That was a rhetorical question," I added, because I could hear her breathing in. "They practically barked at each other and pawed the ground. If there'd been a fire hydrant, Noah would have peed on it."

"I never realized you were such a cosmic hottie."

"Very funny."

She made a sort of snorting noise. "Just watch out. If Noah actually decides he likes you, it'll be like having a giant St. Bernard trying to bring you flowers."

"All Noah's interested in is actually getting his hand up my shirt. Which if I was going to do, it would not be with Noah."

I heard Lily snort again.

"Oh God, does that make me sound awful? I haven't had any *practice* at this."

"Mom says experimentation is healthy, we just have to set good boundaries," Lily said. She managed to quit laughing.

"Is that code for nothing below the waist?"

"I think so."

"Does anybody tell boys things like that, or do they just tell us?"

"Well, they make them carry that egg around. I think that's supposed to give them the idea about consequences."

Jesse had put his egg in his bookbag, where it broke and glued all his notes on *Othello* together. I said, "I don't think consequences occur to boys. And Mom got on me because she thinks Jesse's too old for me. But he hasn't gotten romantic—he was just pissed at Noah. I think."

"How do *you* feel about *Jesse*?" Lily said. "That's the question."

"He makes me a little nervous when he gets intense."

"That may not be a bad thing."

"But I really like him."

"Okay."

"So what would *you* do?" I asked her.

"I read somewhere that what you do in high school has absolutely no impact on your future success and happiness," she said. "I'm banking on that. Unless of course you run off and get married. That would impact it."

Like my mom did. I said, "Maybe that's what Mom's

worried about. That the little acorn hasn't fallen far from the tree."

"Could be. So maybe you don't have to *do* anything about Jesse, Ange. Just lighten up and see what happens."

"I suppose."

"And if Noah keeps on, you can put a dead fish in his locker."

Now that would be a great idea, if I was only a guy. "Okay," I told Lily. "I'll file that one away."

"You'll thank me later."

"I'm thanking you now," I said, and hung up laughing. Lily always makes me feel better.

But apparently she hadn't been talking to my subconscious. It took me a long time to get to sleep because I kept thinking about things, particularly Jesse. Then I had the creepiest dream I've ever had. I was dancing with this cute Asian girl and we were in some kind of bar.

It's strange how in dreams nothing ever strikes you as strange at the time. It seemed perfectly normal to be dancing with a girl in a bar, and everybody else was either a soldier or a little Asian girl in a tight dress. I don't mean young girls, just little compared to the American men. The one I was dancing with came up to my chest. And I was a guy, too. I don't know how I knew, but I didn't have to think about it. The music stopped and we sat down and I bought us each a drink. Hers was just cold tea in a shot glass. And I knew she would go upstairs with me if I gave her ten dollars, and I did. Here's where it gets so strange I don't want to go any further, but I can't get it out of my head. I've never had sex with anybody, and in my dream I had sex with this girl, only I was the guy. It was beyond weird. And I would have said it was probably nothing like the real thing, since I don't have any experience with that except for descriptions in books, except that as soon as I woke up I knew where the dream came from.

The clock said 4:00 a.m. I'd been smoking a cigarette, lying in bed beside this naked girl and smoking a cigarette like they do in old movies. I actually thought I still had the thing in my hand when I opened my eyes. I jumped out of bed and wrapped the sheet around me because I thought the naked girl was still there, too. And then reality sort of settled down around me, like I was coming up out of water, or the air was coming down. I wasn't naked—I had on my frog pajamas and a camisole, and I wasn't a guy, either. I sat back down on the bed with my heart pounding and I didn't go back to sleep for the rest of the night. I'd rather have even the dream about the jungle than be part of somebody else's sex life again.

And I did *not* go over to church and ask Felix about that one. In fact, I was so freaked out that I started wishing I hadn't asked him to Thanksgiving dinner. But I did, and I figured I had until Thursday to forget about sharing his body while he had sex with a bar girl. Dreams always fade out so fast you can hardly remember them the next day, anyway.

———

Not this one, apparently. As soon as we picked Felix up on

Thanksgiving, the whole dream came back into my head in Technicolor. I couldn't even look at him at first.

He didn't seem to notice anything, thank God. "Hi," he said as he climbed into Ben's car. "Nice of you and your folks to invite me. Appreciate it," he added looking over at Ben.

"Glad to have you," Ben said, and Grandma Alice said so, too.

"So you work at Angie's church?" she asked.

"Yes, ma'am," Felix said. He wasn't wearing the ratty bathrobe, I noticed. He had on a suit that was a bit thread-bare but respectable, and white socks with his sandals. His hair was combed and slicked back, and he'd just shaved. I could tell because there were little nicks on his chin. He said, "I take care of the garden and polish up the angels."

Grandma Alice smiled. "It's important to pay attention to the angels," she said. "Then they pay attention to us."

"Yes, ma'am, that's the way I feel about it."

Wuffie's house is a big old stone one in the East End. It used to be all orange groves out there except for the house, and there's still a grove that Wuffie and Grandpa Joe own. The oranges are always just coming ripe this time of year, and so are the pomegranates on the tree by their front door.

Wuffie came bustling out as soon as we got there, with a big white chef's apron on and a spoon in her hand. Grandpa Joe was right behind her. He has a white mustache and looks a little bit like Albert Einstein if Einstein combed his hair. He shook hands with Ben and gave him a wink, which I saw. He shook hands with Felix, too, and then everybody rushed around for a while, taking coats and fixing drinks and putting out bowls of nuts, while Mom and Ben looked like bad actors in an amateur play trying to look normal.

The whole house smelled like turkey cooking, and Wuffie's spaniels were hanging around in the kitchen looking hopeful. Those dogs are so dumb they'll eat buttered cardboard, which Ben and Grandpa Joe proved last Thanksgiving.

Mom and Wuffie went back to the kitchen and I overheard Mom saying, "Mother, this is *my* decision!" and Wuffie saying, "But darling, you are always so *hasty*. Ben is a prize."

"I'm not trying to knock ducks over at the fair."

Wuffie made a "Hmmph!" noise.

Mom said, "Define prize."

"He loves you. He respects you."

"He doesn't." Mom rattled around in a drawer. "Where the hell is the whisk? And since he doesn't, why hang around waiting for the inevitable?"

"You're leaving him before he leaves you?" Wuffie sounded really annoyed. "Sylvia—"

"He thinks my feelings don't matter. So I can see what's coming. So, fine."

"I doubt that," Wuffie said, and I did too. I know why she's mad but I can't see why she thinks it means he doesn't love her.

Then Grandma Alice came in to help and they had to quit arguing.

Ben was talking to Grandpa Joe, and I realized they were expecting me to talk to Felix since I'd invited him. He was looking at a big silver bowl full of pomegranates on the buffet.

"You ever eat one of these?" he asked me, poking them with a finger.

"Yeah. They take forever. You have to peel them and pick the seeds out. It's the seeds you eat."

"I know," he said. "We used to have a tree in the backyard when I was a kid. The seeds look like little rubies and the juice stains your fingers."

"Grandpa Joe fed me some seeds and told me the Persephone story when I was about four. Scared me to death," I said. "I thought I was going to have to go live in the Underworld."

"She ate six seeds, right? And so she had to stay six months in the Underworld after Hades kidnapped her. That idea's even older than the Greeks," Felix told me. "In a lot of cultures, if you eat somewhere you tie yourself to it. And it to you."

Was that what he did in Vietnam? Eat there and tie himself to it? Well, of course you'd have to eat. But eating was a metaphor. Mom's big on metaphor, so I know all about that. Sex, death, and food are all linked up together. I could feel my face burning again as soon as I had that thought. My coloring makes it hard to see me blush (one of life's little compensations), but Felix could tell from my expression that something was wrong.

"Uh, you have any more weird dreams?" he asked.

I snapped my head around. "Why do you ask?"

"Which one was it?" he said.

I kept my eyes on the pomegranates. "Um. In a bar. Um."

He laughed suddenly. I don't think I'd ever heard him laugh before that. He sat down on the sofa and closed his eyes, grinning a huge grin. "I guess it was educational," he said, with his eyes closed.

"Will you shut up?" I hissed. I sat down next to him so I could whisper. "I did *not* want to know that stuff."

"Well, I didn't exactly want you to know it," he whispered back. At least he was being quiet.

"What kind of behavior is that for a saint, anyway?"

"Saints are human."

"All the girl saints were martyred for refusing to marry pagans. They didn't do stuff like that."

"I'm not a girl saint."

"You're not any kind of saint. I don't know why I even said that. Get your dreams out of my head!"

"Angie!" Wuffie called from the kitchen. "Would you and, uh, Felix, set the table for me? Use the good china."

Felix hopped up from the sofa. "Great! Let's go be useful."

I've spent my whole life hanging around Wuffie's house, so I know where everything is. I showed Felix the good dishes in the cabinet and I got out the silver. Wuffie already had the good tablecloth on, so we laid out seven places—Wuffie and Grandpa Joe at each end, and the rest of us two to one side, three to the other. If I could manage it I was going to get Grandma Alice and Felix on one side with me, so Mom would have to sit next to Ben.

Grandpa Joe carried the turkey in and everybody else brought the other stuff. Mom dodged my secret plan and sat down on the far end of the side with three places just as I sat down on the other end and beckoned Felix into the middle seat. So Ben sat across from Mom, but at least she had to look at him.

"Joseph, would you say grace, please?" Wuffie said.

Grandpa Joe grinned. "We are lucky dogs," he said, to which Ben and Mom and I all answered, "Arf!" Wuffie hates that one, but she forgot to tell him not to do it.

Grandma Alice giggled. Grandpa Joe started carving the turkey. It looked like things might be going to go all right, especially when Ben started talking to Grandpa Joe about the Middle East. They don't see eye-to-eye and can make the subject last all night when they get going. In our house, religion and politics are not forbidden topics—they're the usual sources of conversation. Ben says our family motto is, "Choose your side and your subject."

"I don't care whose side you're on or what the history is," Grandma Alice was saying, getting into it too. "There is no such thing as a 'holy' war. War is not holy."

Then Mom jumped in, sort of accidentally landing on Ben's side.

"Do they come to blows?" Felix whispered to me. "Should I watch for flying china?"

"No, they're having fun," I said back. There was no need to whisper. My family is very loud.

They kept it going all the way through pumpkin pie, just like they always do, and on into the kitchen with the dishes. I was having the best time. My family is very opinionated, but they're well read, and we aren't above cheating either. I learned a long time ago that when Ben says that "studies show" something-or-other, you have to ask him if it's a real study or one he just made up because he's convinced studies *would* show that if someone actually did one. He'll tell you if he's made it up, but not unless you ask.

Everyone was bumbling around in the kitchen, scraping plates and waving their arms and generally having a good time, while Cookie and Cupcake, the spaniels, wandered around underfoot waiting for someone to drop something. Grandpa Joe dismembered the turkey carcass and dumped it in the trash, and Wuffie packed the rest of the meat into Tupperware. Mom was washing the good china. Ben sidled up next to her and started loading the dishwasher with the other stuff, and she didn't even glare at him. Grandma Alice and Felix and I got the rest of the things off the table. We'd just folded up the tablecloth when there was one of those sounds that anybody who has a dog knows. We all turned around to look at Cookie, gagging and hacking up blood and gristle on the kitchen floor.

"Oh my God!" Mom dropped the dish sponge.

"Damn it, it looks like she got in the bones." Grandpa Joe pried Cookie's jaws open and Ben stuck his hand down her throat. The garbage can lid was standing open and there were turkey bones all over the floor. I made a dive for Cupcake and fought her for the bone in her mouth. Turkey bones are terribly dangerous for dogs. They can splinter and puncture their intestines.

Ben pulled a bone out of Cookie's throat but she went on gagging.

"Wasn't anybody watching them?" Wuffie said.

"Can's got a lid," Grandpa Joe said. "Apparently the little bitches have learned to open it."

Cookie started staggering around.

Ben stuck his hand down Cookie's throat again and she bit him, sinking a tooth right through his palm. "Goddammit!"

"Do something! She's choking!" Mom cried. Cookie was lying down now and her tongue was turning black.

"She's got to go to the emergency vet," Wuffie said. "Somebody help me with her."

"I got her." Felix knelt down beside Cookie and scooped her up in his arms. She was dribbling blood out of her mouth.

"I'll drive," Mom said. "I know where it is."

"Call me when you get there!" Wuffie said, her hands to her mouth as they went out the door.

Ben looked at his hand and started running water on it from the kitchen faucet.

"I'll get you some antibiotic," Grandpa Joe said.

"Do you think Cupcake ought to go too?" Wuffie asked. Cupcake wagged her tail at the sound of her name, looking dopey and hopeful.

"I don't think she actually ate any," I said, because Wuffie looked so worried. "Maybe we ought to take her, though. Ben and I could go."

"You really think we need to?" Ben asked. He rubbed some of Grandpa Joe's antibiotic into his hand.

"Yes." I got Cupcake's leash and she danced around panting when she saw it. *Ooooh, ride!*

"Dog looks fine to me," Grandpa Joe observed.

"Joe, let them take her, please," Wuffie said.

"Okay, sure. We'll go." Ben got his keys out of his pocket. When we got into the car, Cupcake tried to get in his lap and he shoved her at me. "Christ, what an evening. Hold on to her."

The emergency vet is across the valley, a ten-minute drive. Ben didn't say anything else till we got there. Mom's car was already parked outside and we got Cupcake out of ours and went in. Mom was sitting in the waiting room with Felix, and he had his arm around her. They didn't even spring apart the way guilty couples do in movies. Mom looked up and sniffled. "They're working on her." She looked at Ben's hand, which was still bleeding. "What happened?"

"Bit me," he said. "Apparently you didn't notice."

"Oh, poor little Cookie," Mom said.

"It looked to me like she was having a seizure," Felix said.

Mom said, "Poor little Cookie," again, and Felix squeezed her shoulders and said, "Seizures aren't painful, they just look scary. I've seen some."

Then the vet came out. "We've cleared all the bone

fragments but your dog is still having seizures," she told us. "We don't know why. She growled and snapped at my tech. We're concerned at this point about the possibility of a failed rabies shot."

Ben looked at his hand.

"We'd like your regular vet to hold her for a day or two," the vet said, while Cupcake skittered around the waiting room and peed in the corner. She collared Cupcake. "I'll just give Baby here a quick look, too."

"I wouldn't worry," Felix said to Mom after the vet disappeared with Cupcake. "Stress can trigger seizures, and I'd growl too if I'd been through all that."

Mom nodded supportively. At Felix.

"Good to know," Ben said.

This was so not what I'd had in mind—Ben getting bit by a possibly rabid dog while Mom bonded with Felix over the crisis. My kind of plan works in the movies, but I should have known. If anyone knows the movies are smoke and mirrors, it should be me.

————

It turns out—after a week at the vet and a lot of worried phone calls and urine tests they made us collect because none of the techs wanted to walk her—that Cookie does not have rabies. That's a plus, particularly for Ben, but what Cookie does have is epilepsy, apparently triggered by the stress of the turkey-bone incident. So now she takes phenobarbital to prevent further seizures, which it does, except for times of extreme stress like baths and additional vet visits. Then she lies down and foams at the mouth and twitches on the sidewalk. It completely unhinges Wuffie, who thinks Cookie is going to die each time, so Felix has started coming over to Wuffie's to do things like bathe Cookie and take her for her checkups. Mom picks him up, or he walks there. All the way. He says it gives him time to think. I worry that what he's thinking about is Mom.

I can't wait for Christmas. The house will probably catch fire. In the meantime, there's the Posadas procession.

10

The Monday after Thanksgiving, there was a drawing of
the Posadas stable in my locker. The angels were leaning
down from their sign with brooms, whacking at a donkey with Noah's face that had just pooped on the floor.
I couldn't help snickering even though I knew Noah was
right behind me. It looked just like him. Jesse is *good*.

I heard Noah's locker door slam and shoved the drawing into my folder before he could start anything. I showed
it to Lily at lunch and she cracked up, too. "You're way too
good at that," she told Jesse. "You ought to be doing car-
toons for the *Oak Tree*." That's our school paper.

Jesse gave her an evil grin. "None of my ideas are fit to
print."

Some of his drawings are just wicked, like the one of

Noah, but a lot of them are sweet. He's done two of me as an angel, and one as the Virgin from the Posadas parade. I've quit taping them up on my bedroom wall, though. There are too many, and Ben will start in on me or tell Mom or both.

I told Jesse I'd love a ride home after Posadas rehearsals, to make up for last time.

Father Weatherford has gotten nearly every store in the arcade to let us bring our donkey up to their door. City Hall will let us take the donkey down the sidewalk as long as someone goes along behind us with a shovel. Felix got assigned that job, which he doesn't seem to mind any more than he minds bathing a dog who has fits or cleaning the fifty-year-old crud out of St. Thomas's antique plumbing. I don't understand that very well. Sometimes I think he's trying to pay for something.

Jesse came early on Sunday to watch the rehearsal and brought his sketchpad. He drew the Wise Men and put in some camels behind them. Father Weatherford loved it, so Jesse gave him the sketch. Afterward we went for coffee and he gave me a drawing, too, of Felix leaning on his shovel under the pergola. The leaves of the trees give Felix a kind of shadowy halo and just the faintest suggestion of wings. When Jesse tore it out, I could see pages and pages of mazes in the book behind it, but now the mazes have little people in them. Some of the people have angels' wings, too, and some of them have tails. Not devil tails, more like dog tails. It looked like something out of Hieronymus Bosch. Two of them have heads of wild, curly black hair, one of the winged ones and one of the dog-tailed ones. I hope Jesse's okay over Christmas break.

———

The latest development is that Grandma Alice has decided to make a big dinner for Hanukkah and invite Grandpa Joe, which means that Wuffie and Mom are coming too, of course.

"I don't think Joe's said the prayers since he was twelve," Ben told Grandma Alice, but he wasn't going to argue with her. Me, I think it's another ploy to get Mom and Ben together. I hope nobody chokes on a turkey bone this time. Wuffie accepted fast enough, for all of them. Without asking Mom.

———

But Mom came over without any problem, the first night of Hanukkah. She patted the Todal, who adores her and nearly knocked her over he was so excited. She said how good everything smelled and could she help, but Grandma Alice said she had it all under control, so Mom had to socialize with us like a guest, which she was pretending to be anyway. I asked if she was coming to see me in the Posadas parade.

"Of course. I wouldn't miss it. Whatever persuaded Father Weatherford to use live animals? He must have nerves of steel. Or dementia."

"So, do you want to see me, or just see if something awful happens?" I asked.

Mom grinned. "A little of both." That sounded more like her old self.

"If it does," I said, "I didn't do it," and then Grandma Alice said to come to the table.

The food report: Grandma Alice made matzoh ball soup, and latkes, which are these heavenly pancakes of shredded potatoes, fried in oil. You eat them with sour cream and applesauce, and they are even better than matzoh ball soup. Oil is the big symbol on Hanukkah, since it commemorates the time when the Jews got their temple back from the Romans and there wasn't enough oil to light the holy lamps for longer than one day. The Jews poured in the oil they had, and it miraculously lasted eight days. So Hanukkah lasts eight days, but the big nights are the first and the last. And I would go anywhere for latkes.

Grandma Alice got out her favorite menorah, an antique silver one we gave her for Christmas last year. (Okay, I know that's peculiar, but everybody in our family figures the more chances to give somebody a present, the better.) Instead of holding candles, it hangs on the wall and has little cups for actual oil and wicks. Ben and I hassled with it all day, making a backing for it so it wouldn't get hot and set the drywall on fire.

Grandpa Joe loved it, of course. It's very historical. Not to mention the possibility of its catching on fire. "Ben, I tell you, this is great," he said. "Very traditional Old World. Where did you get it?"

"Antique shop on Fairfax," Ben said.

"Joseph, would you like to say the prayers?" Grandma Alice asked him.

"Watch him," Wuffie said.

"No lucky dogs," Grandma Alice said. She shook a finger at Grandpa Joe. "The real prayers."

"Sure," Grandpa Joe lit the first cup of oil and rattled them off. In Hebrew.

Even Wuffie looked surprised.

"Some things you don't forget," he said, putting his arm around her.

"I thought you weren't religious, Dad," Mom said.

"You don't have to be to remember prayers you heard your whole childhood," Grandpa Joe told her.

"You imprint on things," Wuffie said to Mom. "They stay with you. I've always been grateful to your father for subordinating his things to mine." She smiled at him and leaned her head against his shoulder. I thought maybe she was reminding Mom that Ben had done exactly that for her when he agreed to get married in a church. But I knew that wasn't a selling point with Mom. The thing Mom wants Ben to change for her is not religious.

I think Grandpa Joe and Ben, and even Mom, are kind of generally spiritual people. They're okay with any path to God. But the specifics of religion, the actual ritual, matter to Wuffie and Grandma Alice.

After Grandpa Joe lit the first light, we sat down and scarfed latkes and soup and salmon, and challah that Grandma Alice baked herself, and ruggelah for dessert, these heavenly little crescents made with cream cheese pastry and cinnamon and walnuts and raisins. I swear I would be Jewish for the food.

Mom ate everything and hugged Grandma Alice. She didn't hug Ben.

———

At dress rehearsal this Sunday we got to practice with the donkey, who is really kind of cute, although he smells. He has huge ears and big brown eyes. I have to sit on him sidesaddle, because I wear a long blue gown and a blue cloak with stars, like the Virgin of Guadalupe. Father Weatherford went all-out on costumes this year—no shepherds in their bathrobes. The Three Kings look like sultans with brocade robes and turbans, and the angels all have real feather wings. The wings scared the donkey, but after we let him sniff them he settled down.

I told Jesse not to pick me up this time because I was going Christmas shopping with Lily afterward, and she was waiting for me as we finished up. When she saw me coming on the donkey, she knelt down on the church lawn and crossed herself. "Looking holy!" she said.

"Knock it off." I slid down from the saddle. "I'll whap you with my halo" (which, thank the Virgin herself, we don't have to wear).

Noah took the donkey into the stable and I dug the Baby Jesus out of the straw and laid him in the manger. The angels sang "O Holy Night" and the Three Kings unpacked their invisible camels and knelt down in front of us to present me with three of Noah's mom's jewelry boxes. They sang "We Three Kings of Orient Are" while Father Weatherford glared at them to make sure they didn't put in the line about the rubber cigar.

Friday is the parade, and we're going to do this with live sheep and camels.

————

Lily and I drove into Ventura to shop. I'm a total freak about Christmas. I love the decorations, the cheesy mechanical Santas and singing bears at the mall, the people who put eight reindeer, three wise men, four angels, and Santa in a helicopter on their roof and blow all the fuses trying to light it. I love all of it. Despite the fact that I'm convinced that this Christmas is going to be a complete disaster, I've been obsessing about what to give everyone. Mom is always good with a book of poetry, but I want something that will make her want to come home.

"How about a photograph album?" Lily suggested. "Undermine her with sentiment."

"With pictures of Ben? That's a little blatant."

"No, doofus. Pictures of the three of you, doing things together. Ben just happens to be in them."

"Mmm."

"Music? Who's some singer she likes, who will make her think of Ben? Or go with poetry. How about love poetry?"

"Would any of those work on you?"

"No." Lily turned the car into the mall parking lot. "But I'm a hard sell. Your mom's a romantic. I had her for English, remember?"

"I wish I knew what it is Ben won't take out of that script."

Lily grinned. "Yeah, me too."

"Sometimes I wish I had your parents."

"No, you don't. They'll talk about anything. My parents are a walking case of Too Much Information."

The mall was piping "White Christmas" into the parking lot through a speaker in the palm trees. The sun was out and it was at least 70 degrees. I wonder what a white Christmas is like. We went in and cruised, and when Lily wasn't looking I got her the new Norah Jones CD. I got Felix a coffeemaker, which Mom had agreed to go in on.

A store selling suncatchers and incense had a row of bronze figures in the window and Lily pointed a finger at one. I peered in at him, a little man with an elephant's head, sitting lotus-fashion.

"For your mom," Lily said. "He's Ganesh, the remover of obstacles."

"That might backfire," I said. "He might remove Ben." But they had a little brass Buddha that I thought she'd like, and Buddha is all about being at peace with things, according to Mom. That's what I mean about Mom being kind of a generalist, religiously. I bought her the Buddha, thinking that maybe he could tell her to be at peace with Ben.

For Ben I had a list of geek presents to pick from, like wireless mice and flash drives. I'd consulted Wuffie on

Grandpa Joe, who is always impossible to shop for, and bought him a koi for his koi pond, which the water-garden people will keep till he picks it up. I'm going to wrap a plastic one for him if I can find one. I also went to Body Works and got gardenia hand cream for Wuffie and Grandma Alice.

Jesse of all people was in there, staring at the body wash.

He spotted Lily first. "Reindeer! Come and help me."

"What are you looking for?" I followed her over.

"Oh." He looked at me wildly, the way guys do when they're on bubble-bath-and-pink-ribbon overload. "My, uh, mom..."

I showed him the gardenia hand cream. "My grannies both love this."

"Is that an old lady smell? She's not... uh, what do *you* like?"

"Well, my mom likes the gardenia, too, but these are my faves." I pointed at the coconut lime and the freesia. "Does your Mom take baths or showers?"

He stared at me. "I don't know."

"'Cause the bubble bath is better than the body wash if she takes baths, but it's no good in the shower."

"I told her she should come with me," he said. "I mean, not her come with me to shop for her, but..." He trailed off, grabbed the coconut lime body wash, and ran off.

For some reason, Lily was cracking up.

((

The camels arrived Friday morning in a horse trailer. They *do* spit. They spat at Father Weatherford while the handlers unloaded them. He looked revolted, but he blessed them. There were three of them and the handler tied them to a palm tree beside the stable, where they ate some thatch off the roof and scratched their butts on the tree trunk. We put the sheep in a pen and tied the goats up inside the stable, where they ate the straw from under Baby Jesus.

The procession was actually pretty cool. We waited until after dark, and the older angels carried candle lanterns. The candles glowed on their feathers and the magi's crowns, and on my cloak, and we looked like a stained glass window. That's what Felix said. He wore a shepherd costume and carried the shovel.

The stores were all lit up with Christmas lights and some of them gave us cookies after we sang. There were a lot of people lined up along Ayala Avenue to watch us, especially around the arcade and on the sidewalk across the street. My whole family was there, naturally, and I saw Jesse with his mom and his little brother and sister, and Lily and her mom and dad. Everyone had cameras, and the flashes made about as much light as the lanterns. Jesse waved at me and held his up to show me he'd taken my picture.

It actually got cold that night. You never know in Southern California; we're as likely to be wearing shorts at Christmas as not. When we got to the stable, Noah kind of snuggled up next to me and put his arm around me, like Joseph would for Mary. I was glad of it because we were supposed to pose for half an hour, and once I got off the donkey, who was pretty warm, I started to shiver, even in my starry cloak. Then I felt Noah's hand sliding along through the layers of the cloak into my robe.

"Stop it!" I hissed at him. I wanted to smack him but I couldn't, because all kinds of people were watching us. Anyway, we were supposed to be a *tableau vivant*, a bunch of living statues (except for the camel who was still scratching his butt on a tree). "Quit it!" I said.

"Aww." He looked at me sideways without moving his head much. He has this goofy grin.

"Remember your relationship with God," I whispered.

"I'm more interested in my relationship with you."

"You don't *have* any relationship with me," I said. I was getting exasperated. "And if you don't move your hand

I will tear it off and stuff it up your butt just as soon as this pageant is over!" And then I winced because I was a little too loud and the lady who was taking our picture heard me.

"*You* aren't going to heaven," Noah said out of the side of his mouth.

I couldn't help a snort of laughter. That did it. One of the shepherds giggled just because it's contagious. Missy Escobar's shoulders started shaking while she tried to hold her box of frankincense still, and then everyone was cackling, even though they didn't know what at—just at us kneeling there in the cold, pretending to be Biblical figures even though the head angel got caught smoking pot behind the gym last week, and two of the shepherds are on probation at school for exploding their chemistry experiment on purpose, not to mention Noah, who is perpetually grounded or in trouble.

Father Weatherford came whisking up in his vestments and glared at us, and we tried to stop. We really did. But sometimes you just can't. Life is just too funny, or maybe too scary, and you know you're not holy, and the camel is so silly looking, and the more you try to behave, the more you just want to lie down on the floor and howl. Untied dogs for sure. We got it back together eventually, but I know Father Weatherford felt we'd let him down, so we stayed as still as we could for the next ten minutes until he gave the signal and the angels sang "O Holy Night" again, and everyone applauded.

Mom came up afterward to tell me how beautiful it all was. I thought she was going to give me the Serious Talk about Acting More Maturely, but she didn't. Then when Ben came over, she started talking to Felix as if she just hadn't happened to notice Ben. While Ben, on the other hand, definitely noticed them. So I was grateful when Jesse came over to show me the pictures he'd taken of us. I had to stay for the cast party afterward, and Father Weatherford invited Jesse to stay, too. He probably thought he'd be a good example for us. I thought the last thing Jesse would want to do would be go to a church social with a bunch of kids, but he said sure.

Father Weatherford and some of the Youth Group parents had laid out a spread of Christmas cookies and hot spiced cider in the parish hall. Someone brought marshmallows and graham crackers and chocolate so we all flopped down on the floor by the fireplace with our plates and cups and made s'mores. Jesse sat next to me. He had to keep his left leg out straight at a weird angle, and the android-looking calf part of it stuck out, so of course the little kids all wanted to know what it was. I thought he might get mad, but he actually pulled up his cuff some more and showed it to them. When they asked too many questions, he taught them how to toast s'mores.

Father Weatherford put Christmas carols on and we ate and listened to "It Came Upon a Midnight Clear." The firelight made little flickering orange lights and shadows that danced across everyone's face. It was beautiful and magical, so naturally Noah started waving his charred drippy marshmallow around like an idiot, saying, "Look, it's Char Man!" The marshmallow was all black and starting to split in two. He poked it in the fire again and it went up in flames.

"There is no such person," Missy Escobar said. "And don't get that in my hair."

Noah made a horrible face at her. "You don't want to find out some dark night."

One of the littlest kids said, "What's Char Man?"

"You don't know?"

Char Man is a local legend. Almost every kid over the age of five has heard it. So Noah told him. "There was this awful fire, like, way back in the eighties. It was in all the papers. Some guy's tractor started it in the brush down in the river-bottom. And there were, like, all these houses down there. And there was this one house where this old dude lived with his brother. The old guy was real old, and his brother was just seventeen."

"How could he be seventeen if his brother was old?" Missy asked. She rolled her eyes at me, like, *dork*.

"Their father had two wives, and the second one had the kid when their old man was real old himself," Noah said. "Don't interrupt, nonbeliever. So, the younger brother took care of his older brother who'd been wounded in some war and was messed up. He was in a wheelchair."

I couldn't help flicking an eye at Jesse to see if that bothered him. He was fixing another marshmallow for one of the little kids and didn't seem to notice. But he has this little tic beside his eye that he gets when something upsets him.

"Then the fire started. And the dude in the wheelchair got trapped."

The little kids all gasped. "What happened?" one of them asked.

"He burned to death." Noah looked at them all solemnly. He's a pretty good storyteller. "The younger brother tried to get him out, but the flames were too hot. The younger brother ran around and around the house trying to get in, and he could hear the old guy in there screaming the whole time."

I felt Jesse twitch, like he was flinching, and I remembered Felix's dream about the boats burning up on the river. Jesse was staring at the fire now.

"Then the roof fell in." Noah smacked his hands together and blew his breath out fast. "And the fire was coming down the canyon."

The little kid clapped his hand over his mouth.

"They never found him."

"Who, the guy in the wheelchair?" someone asked.

"The younger brother. He'd waited too long and he couldn't get out of the canyon."

"He died?"

Noah shook his head. "He's still out there. Lots of people have seen him. His face is half burned away and where one of his eyes ought to be, there's just this glob of jelly, like a marshmallow." He held the drippy marshmallow up to his eye and hung his tongue out the side of his mouth. "He couldn't get his brother out, see, and he went crazy. He stayed down in the chaparral and scrub brush, eating animals that had been burned in the fire. He's still there."

"Well, what does he eat now?" Missy asked.

"Whatever he can catch. Raw."

"Eeeww."

"He caught this girl who went out hiking alone last summer."

"He did not," Missy said. "It would have been in the paper."

"Her parents hushed it up. What was left of her was so gross, they didn't want anyone to see it."

"That's disgusting."

"He runs down deer," Noah said. "I saw a chicken he caught once. There was nothing left but the feet and some feathers. He ate it, guts and all."

"That was coyotes," Missy said.

"Naw. It was Char Man. The fire couldn't kill him, so nothing will. He keeps coming back to where his house used to be."

I don't believe in Char Man, but that didn't stop me from getting the creepy feeling that something was actually out there. I scooted a little closer to Jesse and he laughed as if he knew why, but the laugh sounded forced.

"God. I'd forgotten all about Char Man," he said. "I was raised on that story. I heard it at Boy Scout camp."

"It's so stupid, but it gives me the creeps," I said.

"Fire does that." Jesse looked back to where the flames were melting marshmallows into gobs of goo. "It … transforms things."

I think there was a fire when Jesse got hurt. He didn't get burned, but I think someone did. I can't ask him. I just can't.

———

Afterward I was on trash detail, and Jesse stayed to help me and drive me home. Mom and Ben assumed I would walk, so they didn't have a chance to say not to go with Jesse.

It's amazing how much stuff religious, supposedly civilized people will drop. We cleaned up drink cups from the Frosty and tons of gross cigarette butts and hamburger wrappers. We bagged it up with the straw from the stable floor and lugged it all out to the dumpster in back. There was an actual coyote nosing around the dumpster, with a hamburger wrapper in his mouth. In the middle of town. He took off when he saw us.

"Nervy little shits, aren't they?" Jesse said. He tossed the garbage bag into the dumpster. "Here, give me yours."

I handed it to him and he tossed it too. Then he rummaged in his coat pocket. He pulled out something wrapped in tissue paper and handed it to me. "I asked Reindeer. She said you take showers."

I stood there like an idiot, trying to figure out what he meant.

Jesse tapped a finger on the tissue paper package. "Open it. I didn't want to give it to you in there in front of all those idiots."

It was the coconut lime body wash from Body Works. I smiled at him. "Thank you. This is my favorite."

"I'm glad you like it. You looked great tonight in the parade," he said.

"I felt like an imposter," I said. "I'm not holy."

"You are to me," Jesse said. Real quietly, so I almost

didn't hear him. "When things get bad, I'll think about you in that starry cloak. You'll be my talisman."

I was thinking about what Felix said about the time he saw the Virgin, and whether anything that awful had happened to Jesse, and also about whether it would be a good idea to be somebody's talisman, when Jesse put his hands on my shoulders and bent down and kissed me. He was kind of tentative about it, as if he didn't know what I might do.

I kissed him back. I can't say I haven't been wondering what it might be like to kiss Jesse.

He didn't get handsy like Noah would have, he just held me. And after a minute he stepped back and said, "Okay, I think that's probably enough. You make me forget how young you are."

That kind of annoyed me. "I'm almost sixteen."

He laughed. A nice laugh, but he laughed. "You're an innocent. I'd better watch out."

"You'd be surprised," I said, thinking about the dream about the girl in the bar. But if anything, that dream has made me decide I'm *not* ready for sex. The details of it have faded a bit, the way dreams do; thank God, because although I've read that everyone has weird sexual dreams, *that* one is not one I want hanging around in my head. And I was absolutely not going to explain it to Jesse. So I said, sort of prissily, "I have read about these things in books," and he laughed again.

Now I really can't stand it that I won't see him at school until January.

12

Wuffie has invited Felix to Christmas dinner. Which we absolutely have to go to Wuffie's house for, all of us, for the sake of the child—who is me. After what happened on Thanksgiving, I'm not so sure it's a great plan. Felix will probably save Mom from a charging bull or something.

Mom decided that Ben and Grandma Alice and I ought to spend the night at Wuffie's on Christmas Eve, so that the child will have both parents together on Christmas morning. I think Felix talked her into it and I don't know if that's good or bad—if he's been interceding, or if Mom is trying to figure out how they will all be civilized for my sake once she and Ben are divorced. I asked Ben whether, if they actually get divorced, he can get *any* custody of me, and he just shrugged and looked sad.

"Don't you *care*?" I asked him.

"About you? Of course I do, Angelfish."

"About *Mom*!"

He sighed. "Yes, I care."

"Then why don't you take that thing out of your script?" I figured it was worth a shot.

He raised an eyebrow at me. "That thing?"

"Whatever it is she didn't want you to say. She wouldn't tell me what it is. Why don't you just *not*?"

He made that noise he makes when he's irritated, a kind of click with his teeth. "Because there is only a certain point to which I'm willing to be bullied."

"Bullied? But you're writing about *her*!"

"Angie, you don't know everything."

"Then tell me!"

"It's none of your business."

"Yes, it is! You're getting a divorce! Maybe."

"That doesn't make it your business."

"Who else's is it?" I demanded.

"Mine and Sylvia's," Ben said. "As I would think would be obvious."

"And I'm just some … some … ping-pong ball to bat back and forth between you?" I said. "Like a—a pawn?"

"Except that no one's fighting over you," Ben pointed out. "You are not tragically featured in the tabloids yet."

"All right," I admitted. "Hokey dialog." And mixed metaphor, Mom would have said. "But I really hate this."

"I know. But if you have any *Parent Trap*–style shenanigans up your sleeve, ditch them," he warned me.

"I was planning to get you and Mom snowbound together in an isolated cabin so you could meet cute all over again," I said (this is the plot of one of Ben's movies). "But it doesn't snow here." I stomped out.

———————

So on Christmas Eve we went to Wuffie's, and Mom slept in her old room with me, and Grandma Alice slept in the guest room, and Ben slept on the sofa.

I wondered what Mom and Ben were going to do about presents for each other. When I asked, earlier, Ben said, "A tiara," and Mom said, "An exploding cigar," so I gave up.

Mom was whistling "Angels We Have Heard on High" while we got undressed and I climbed into one of the twin beds. The other one still has her old stuffed animals on it, and she picked up a rabbit and looked at it.

"I don't know why Mother doesn't throw these out," she said.

"Maybe they remind her of when you were a kid," I said. "She probably gave you most of them."

"Actually, my first husband gave me this one," Mom said, and tossed it back onto the bed. Then she pulled the covers back and flipped the whole batch of them onto the floor. She started whistling again.

"Mom?" I whispered.

She stopped whistling.

"Did you love him?"

"Oh, darling." A long pause. "I expect I did. He was very

sweet, and he really wanted to take care of me. Until it went to hell." Another pause. "I'm not still grieving over him, if that's what you're thinking."

"Then why are you miserable?"

"I'm not."

"Are too," I said, turning over and punching my pillow into shape.

The Todal, who we had brought with us, padded in and flopped down beside my bed with a long sigh. The light went out and I heard Mom get into bed. "Go to sleep and wait for Santa Claus," she said.

―――――――

They gave each other chocolate. Honestly, it was like those gift exchanges in grammar school where you draw names to be somebody's secret Santa. On the other hand, Mom gave me the sweater I've been drooling over and Ben gave me a framed lobby poster from *Pirates of the Caribbean* with Orlando Bloom's autograph. Ben has connections. Wuffie and Grandpa Joe gave me a ring with a tiny diamond in it that was Wuffie's mother's, and a card with a picture of a T-Bird on it and a note inside that said, *This card may be exchanged on your 16th birthday for a real car (used, 2 to 5 years old) from a list of safe, dependable models.* I'll be sixteen in April. I hugged them both, jumping up and down like an idiot.

"Wheels! Wheels! Wheels!" I shrieked, nearly falling over the Todal, who was asleep in the sun in a pile of spaniels.

"Angie, stop it, you'll break something!" Mom was laughing.

I unwrapped my present from Lily, which I'd been saving, and found the little elephant-headed god, Ganesh. "Good work," I told Ganesh, because he'd already removed one obstacle in my life with Wuffie's present. If I did have to come live here with Mom, I wouldn't have to ride my bike to town. And I could see Ben when I felt like it.

And then Noah Michalski came to the door and handed *me* a box of chocolate. When the doorbell rang, I thought it was going to be Felix and I stood there looking stupid while Noah held out the box, which wasn't wrapped but had the little gold cord thingy the store puts on them, and a tag.

"Dude, what's *that*?" he asked as the Todal came to the door, too.

I said, "That's my dog," and shoved the Todal back into the house. There was a car in the driveway. "Did you drive over here by yourself?"

"No, I have an invisible mother in the car. She won't notice. She's busy burning the turkey."

"You want to come in?" *And get stared at by my family?* I didn't know what to do with him.

"No, that's okay," he said, looking over my shoulder at my assembled relatives, who were all looking at him but pretending not to, like really bad amateur detectives. "I just wanted to bring you this."

"Well, thank you," I said.

"Well, like, Merry Christmas," Noah said, and got in his mom's Toyota and drove over Wuffie's geraniums.

When I went back in, they had all decided to be tactful and were making coffee in the kitchen or pretending to check their email. Mom and Ben were standing in the doorway to the hall where the bedrooms are, talking. Ben's face looked tight, the way it does when he's mad or sad, and Mom had two tears rolling down her cheeks. They both smiled when they saw me, fake smiles like demented manga characters.

"Was that Noah Michalski?" Mom asked, as if she thought maybe it had been a door-to-door evangelist instead.

"No, it was Noah Michalski with a box of drugstore candy his mother made him buy me, thanks to you discussing me with everyone you meet."

They both snorted with laughter. I just glared at them to make it clear it wasn't funny. *Thanks. Glad my private life can take your minds off your divorce.*

I went into the kitchen, where Wuffie was making tamales. That's the other food I will kill for. They're a total pain to make and she only does it at Christmas. She was just putting them on to steam in their little cornhusk jackets and I inhaled blissfully. "Thanks for the car."

"Grandpa will go with you. And no sports cars. Or driving around with boys by yourself. You're too young for a boyfriend."

Okay, first of all, I'm fifteen *and a half* and I know girls younger than me who are pregnant. Or were. But that's probably not the thing to say to Wuffie. And anyway, "Noah Michalski is not my boyfriend," I said. I saw no need to mention any other names.

Besides the tamales, Wuffie made rib roast so there

were bones we could actually give to the dogs, and nobody choked and had any emergency. The Christmas tree sparkled, and we played Christmas carols and talked about the war. Not cheerful exactly, but on everyone's mind, although I kept getting sidetracked thinking about Jesse.

Finally Mom said, "War, war, that's all you think about, Dick Plantagenet!" which is a quote from our favorite awful old movie, *King Richard and the Crusaders*, and everyone cracked up.

"I saw that!" Felix said. "On the Late, Late, Terrible Movie Channel."

Then we all got silly thinking up words for groups of things that don't have names but ought to, like a cheese of bad movies, or a conviction of judges.

"Department store Santa Clauses," Ben said. "A beard."

"Prom dresses," I said. "A slink."

Felix said, "A goof of spaniels." Cupcake was sitting on his feet waiting for him to drop something.

"A yawp of poets." That was Ben.

Mom said, "A despair of English teachers."

"Oh, no," Wuffie said. "Surely not that bad." She scratched Cupcake's head and made a face. "Ugh. A suction of ticks."

"Gross," I said while I helped Wuffie take Cupcake into the kitchen to deal with that. But it was so great, just like Christmas always has been, with everyone sitting around the table getting silly and being happy. And when we sang carols Mom and Ben harmonized just like they used to, without even thinking about it.

13

The family coziness didn't last. I should have known it wouldn't. We'd barely gotten home before Mom and Ben were on the phone, back to arguing about whatever it was they'd been arguing about before dinner. Grandma Alice and I could hear Ben through his office door. You could tell by his voice he was mad, and every so often a few words surfaced: "... a screw loose ... No, I am not ... didn't bother you when *he* ... God *damn* it!" We heard him slam the phone into the cradle and I winced. Grandma Alice looked embarrassed, as if she was still responsible for him.

I was so mad I was almost crying. I had such high hopes when everything was so nice at dinner, but I should have known. They're both morons. They ruin everything. Am I going to turn out like that, too? Like Mom, somebody who can't settle on one man and makes all her husbands so crazy that they swear at her? I think it may have been Felix that Ben was mad about. But if it wasn't Felix, it would be something else. Why can't she just be happy? Why does she get these fits, like some kind of itch, that she has to go start a totally different life, that the one she's got isn't any good anymore? I'm probably just lucky she doesn't decide she wants a different kid, too. Maybe that's what's wrong with me—some genetic weirdness from Mom that makes me have other people's dreams, like I can't settle down in my own skin.

I haven't told anybody but Felix about the dreams. And God, of course, but He hasn't given me any advice. Maybe I'm just as batshit crazy as Felix is. Maybe I ought to tell someone before I start wandering around with a saucepan on my head or something. I could start with Lily, I guess; she could tell me whether she thinks I really need a shrink or am just upset about Mom. And why would being upset about Mom make me dream about being in some foreign country where they're shooting people? Or worse yet, being a guy having sex with a girl. Oh God, I don't even want to think about that one. Go away! Get out of my head!

––––––

I called Lily the next day to see if we could hang out at her place because I was totally sick of watching Ben walk around the house with his own personal thundercloud following him, and she came and picked me up. Lily's house has all this wild Nepalese and Tibetan art and embroideries all over. They have a big silver head on the coffee table that Lily says is Mahakala, the Face of Wrathful Compassion. I thought that pretty much summed up what I'm feeling about Ben and Mom right now—wrathful compassion. Emphasis on the wrathful.

We got some chips and yogurt and a bowl of hummus out of the refrigerator and took it to her room. She put on the Norah Jones CD I gave her and I told her about the dreams. I left out the part about Felix claiming he's a saint. I figured the dreams were enough.

"So, am I crazy?"

Lily pointed her yogurt spoon at me. "It's always a possibility."

"That is so not what I wanted to hear."

She swung her head side to side. Her hair looks like a curtain when she does that. I wish mine would. "I don't think you're crazy, if you want to get serious about this," she said. "Maybe you've just got too much going on in your life right now, and stuff kind of runs from one place to another."

"My head leaks?"

"Possibly."

"That's reassuring. Seriously, Christmas was weird. On top of my parents fighting, Noah gave me a present. I know his mom made him, because my mom told her how he trashed me, and *his* mom told *my* mom he's sorry. God!"

"*Noah* gave you a present?"

"Drugstore chocolate."

"Imaginative."

"Come on. This is Noah."

"No one else?"

I bounced on the bed and forgot all about the dreams. "Yes, Miss Too-Smart. Jesse did. And don't tell me you're surprised, because you told him what to get me. And what's more, he kissed me!"

Lily looked interested at that. She stopped with a spoonful of yogurt halfway to her mouth and smiled. "I *thought* he had a crush on you."

"And I've got to get him something, but I don't know what. What can I give him?"

"Music?"

"I don't know what he likes."

"iTunes?"

"Oh God that's lame. That's like a gift certificate."

"Art supplies?"

"Maybe." I bit my lip. "But what if he thinks I'm trying to get him to make art because I think it's therapy for him, or—"

"Cologne?"

"What if he thinks that's coming on too strong? Is cologne too personal?"

"Are you getting a tad bit obsessive here? You sound like someone who takes those quizzes in *Seventeen*. I say this as a friend."

"Lily, the cutest, most interesting guy in the school just kissed me. Could you please get into the spirit? Imagine ... who?

Who do you like? Imagine whoever it is just kissed you and gave you a Christmas present."

"Um. What we have here is a divergence in point of view," Lily said.

"Huh?"

"Divergence. Difference. To be honest, there isn't anybody in that school I would touch with a toasting fork."

"Well, thanks for the testimonial on my taste."

Lily grinned. "Mom says I'm an old soul. I have to wait for the boys to grow up."

I thought about the way Ben was acting. "Good luck with that."

"You might want to wait, too," she suggested.

I looked stubborn. "Not going to."

She grinned again. "I expect not."

That's why I like Lily.

She did say she doesn't believe I'm actually crazy, so we switched to the subject of New Years' Eve. Some friends of Mom and Ben are having a party, and I'm invited too because apparently they have kids my age, so I think I'll go to that. I want to see what Mom and Ben do at midnight. I hope it's not try to kill each other. When I asked Mom why they were both going to the same party, she said that half the people in Ayala used to be married to the other half, and if people didn't go to parties just because their former partners would be there, no one would be able to go anywhere. I so do not want to end up like that. Maybe I should just be a nun. On the other hand, I don't want to end up like *that* either. Particularly not now.

I miss how I used to go and tell this stuff to St. Felix the statue, and he would just listen while I talked to him. I don't know why I don't ask Father Weatherford where the statue is. I think I'm afraid of him saying "What statue?" And even if I did find it again, I wouldn't ever be sure who I was really talking to anymore. Anyway, Felix (the one who's walking around) is part of the problem now, rescuing dogs and getting invited to dinner. And I started that, which is even worse.

In the meantime, I am going to get Jesse some good brushes at the art store. Therapy aside, that seems to strike the right balance between friend and girlfriend. A sort of present-from-someone-you-have-kissed-once present.

———————

New Year's Eve is like the full moon squared—everyone goes nuts. Ben, of all people, asked me if I thought he looked okay while we were getting ready for the party. And then Mom called me up to ask what *she* should wear. Usually Mom is more worried about what I'm wearing and whether it's appropriate, which means not too low on top or too short on the bottom, or black. I'd bought a killer dress that is all three, but she didn't even remember to ask me. And when we got there and she saw it, she didn't even say anything. She was too busy pretending she hadn't noticed Ben and making sure he could notice her, in a black and silver dress that was even more outrageous than mine.

There was a huge crowd, with a caterer passing around trays of little cheese puffs and things in phyllo dough. I felt very glamorous in my dress, but it was kind of a waste until Jesse came in with his parents.

Everyone in Ayala knows everyone, like Mom says, so I wasn't completely surprised. I'd really been hoping Jesse would come, so I'd brought his present just in case. Up until he got there, there were only two twelve-year-old girls and the hosts' kid, Gregory, who is thirteen; you could tell his parents were making him socialize with us when he'd rather be playing video games. That is not my definition of "kids your age, dear."

As soon as Jesse came in he was mobbed with people patting him on the back. I lost track of him until he popped up beside me.

"Hey, Ange," he said. "Can I hide behind you?"

He still had his down jacket on and he looked like he was trying to hide in it.

"Who's after you?" I asked him.

His mouth twisted. "The anti-war committee and the pro-war committee, and the committee to tell me what a fine young man I am and see if they can't enlist me in their cause."

"Oh. Then I'll hide you."

"You want a glass of wine?"

That made me feel extremely grown-up, but I said, "I don't think they'll give me one."

"They'll give me one," Jesse said. "Stay here."

He wriggled his way through the crowd around the bar

and came back with a glass of wine in each hand. "White okay?"

"You aren't twenty-one either," I said when he handed it to me, but I didn't hand it back.

"War hero." He grinned. It was kind of a nasty grin, but then it softened up. He said, "I was hoping you'd be here."

I scoped out the room to see if Mom or Ben was noticing me, then took a sip of wine.

"Come in here." Jesse took my elbow and we slid past a knot of people into the sunroom, where Gregory and the girls were watching a giant orange on TV, counting down to midnight. They didn't pay any attention to us.

"Give me that coat," I said. "You look like you're getting ready to explore the Alps."

He took it off and I handed him my wine. "Hold this for me and look like they're both yours if Mom comes by. I have something I want to get for you." I took his coat to the bedroom where everyone else's were piled on a bed and grabbed his Christmas present out of the pocket of mine.

When I got back to the sunroom, he was standing in a corner with a glass in each hand trying to look invisible. "Merry Christmas." I handed him the package.

"I didn't mean you had to get *me* something!"

"I know you didn't," I said. "Did it ever occur to you, maybe I *wanted* to?"

"Actually, no," he said. "My social skills aren't that finely tuned." He opened it and smiled a big smile. I was glad I hadn't gone for the cologne. "Wow. These are great. And I really need them. I'm hell on brushes."

I know. I've watched him jab them into the paper when he's mad. Probably not tactful to mention that.

He wrapped them back up and stuck them in his shirt pocket where they looked like a giant Christmas-wrap cigar. Then he looked me up and down and said, "I really like you in that dress."

"I like me in this dress, too," I said, grinning at him. "It makes me feel older."

He put his hand on my shoulder. "It's a dangerous dress. You're still a youngster, even if you are about the only person I can talk to who just listens and doesn't think I'm a freak."

"You're not a freak," I said encouragingly.

"Yeah, well, I'm not real stable either," he said.

I'd been talking about the missing leg, not what was going on in his head. I tried to think of the right thing to say. "It must be hard coming back to school, when the rest of us are so much younger, and really clueless."

"That's why I hang out with you."

"Because I'm clueless?"

"Because you're not putting anything on. All the senior girls are trying to be grown up, like they know everything, and I just want to grab them by their necks and say, 'You don't know anything, you stupid *bitch*.'"

"Mmm." I really didn't know what to say to that, so I took another sip of wine and tried to look less like a youngster. The Christmas tree in the corner was all sparkly. It reflected off my wine glass, and I could feel the wine making my head just a little swimmy and then Jesse leaned down and kissed me again. It made me feel grown-up, like this was important and real, until Gregory turned around and saw us and said, "Aw, get a room!" I was embarrassed, but Jesse just grinned at Gregory like he didn't care.

Then, before we could figure out a better place to go, the woman who writes the "People" column for the valley weekly bubbled up to Jesse, like a border collie cutting a sheep out of the herd, and I had to leave him there looking irritated at her. He grabbed my hand and put her on hold for a second, first. "Don't get lost, okay?" he said.

"Okay."

After that I spent most of the party making nice to my parents' friends, talking about where I might want to go to college (I have no clue), and was I going to be a teacher or poet like Mom (I can confidently say no), and how nice we all looked in the Posadas parade. I told Mom how cool her black and silver dress looked. Mom gave my dress a good look then and raised her eyebrows nearly up into her red hair, which was full of silver spangles. Then she shrugged and took another glass of champagne off a tray.

When the bells rang at midnight, Jesse slipped into the circle next to me and squeezed my hand while we all sang "Auld Lang Syne." With everybody watching, he didn't kiss me again, but he said, "Let's do something tomorrow. I'll call you."

"Sure," I said. "And, uh, I'm glad you like the brushes."

I probably sounded like a goon, but he doesn't seem to mind.

After Jesse left with his parents, I grabbed Ben and said, "Are you ready to go? I'm really tired."

He looked kind of surprised and scanned the room. I saw his eye light on Mom, who was standing by the sunroom door, watching him over the rim of her glass. He pointed at me and I saw her nod. "Sure," he said to me. "Come on then, if you're beat. Let's get you home. I'm surprised. I thought you'd outlast the old fogies."

"I got up early," I said.

————

I put on my pajamas, climbed into bed, and hit Lily's number on my cell.

"Of course he liked the brushes. I told you you were obsessing," Lily said. She was at the Art Center folk dancing. I could hear "Hava Nagila" playing in the background.

"We're going to go out somewhere, tomorrow."

"How's your mom going to like that?"

"Mmmm. I haven't got that far." That might be tricky. "But I'll think of something." I'm pretty sure that if Jesse just has someone to care about him, he can get past all the stuff in his head from the war, and people will relax. Maybe that's what Felix didn't have—someone to love him. I wish he could find somebody, as long as it's not Mom.

And after I hung up with Lily, Jesse actually came over

and tapped on my window. When I opened it and poked my head out, he put his elbows up on the sill.

"I couldn't stand to just call. I had to see you again."

I leaned on the sill from the other side till our foreheads touched, and he kissed me. I said, "It's nice to see you again, too."

"Want to go to the movies tomorrow?"

"Um, to be honest, my parents may not like it."

"Am I too old or too crazy?"

"Both, probably," I whispered, and we started giggling like idiots. I'm not even sure why.

"We'll just have to sort of sneak up on them, then," Jesse said. "What would be a nice innocent date?"

"Bookstore," I said. "I'll meet you at Bert's." Bert's is never closed, even on New Year's.

"Two o'clock," Jesse said. He boosted himself up on the sill and kissed me again, and then he disappeared into the darkness. I heard a car start up.

I went to sleep thinking about Jesse, just sliding into this happy fog, and I didn't have any of Felix's dreams. I did dream I was trying to wrap a wet fish up in tissue paper and the paper kept tearing. God knows what that means.

What woke me up was a noise in the living room. I squinted at the clock. It was 3:30 a.m. My room is at the opposite end of the house from Ben's and Grandma Alice's, with the living room in between. The Todal wasn't barking, but I was still scared. I know the kind of noise the Todal makes clicking around the floor at night, and this wasn't it.

This sounded like a person—someone being careful in the dark—and it wasn't Ben's footsteps, either.

I slid out of bed and into the hall. I don't know what I thought I was going to do, but I got to the living room just as whoever it was clicked the front door open, probably making off with Ben's laptop. I switched on the light.

No wonder the Todal hadn't barked. It was Mom, with her shoes and her bra in her hand and her dress on inside out.

14

I didn't say anything, just stood there gawking at her. And the next morning on the phone she pretended she hadn't seen me, which is ridiculous because I'd turned the light on.

"What were you doing wandering around in the middle of the night anyway?" she asked.

"What were *you* doing?"

"What I was doing isn't any of your business." She sounded like she had a headache. I'll bet she had a lot of champagne at that party.

"When are you moving back home?" I asked.

"I'm not. What gave you that idea?"

"Oh come on, Mom. Your hair looked like you

combed it with an eggbeater, and your dress was on inside out."

I could hear her pouring coffee. "What if it was?"

"You can't divorce Ben and then start hooking up with him!" I said indignantly.

"Angie, this is not the time to talk about it. My head hurts."

"You have a hangover."

I was using the house phone and Ben appeared and took it out of my hand. "Good morning, Sunshine," he said into it. I couldn't hear what Mom said, but he laughed and hung up.

"I don't understand you!" I said.

"You don't have to."

"Are you and Mom getting back together?"

"Not at the moment."

That's what I mean about New Year's Eve making people go nuts. So I gave up on them and spent an hour trying to decide what to wear to meet Jesse at Bert's. I finally settled on my new sweater and my black velveteen pants. In another miraculous event, my hair looked perfect.

Jesse was waiting for me when I got there. He bought us both a coffee and we sat at a table under an oak tree. He turned his chair so its back was to a shelf of books. I've noticed that he always sits with his back to the wall. It was a beautiful day, about sixty degrees out and the sky looked like it had just been washed.

"I found something I bet you'll like," Jesse said. He pulled a book out of his backpack. "I already bought it."

It was a book about the Day of the Dead, with lots of photos of skeleton figures—a Day of the Dead bride dancing in her bones and a white veil, skeleton cowboys riding skeleton horses, a skeleton doctor with a stethoscope. There was even a skeleton teacher reading something out of a book, one hand up in the air. I wanted to paste a wild red wig on her and give her to Mom. "This is great," I said. I started to give it back to him but he shook his head. "Nah. It's for you."

I was embarrassed. "This is the third thing you've given me. Counting the Duchess."

He said, "I like to give you things."

I wound a piece of hair around my finger.

"You have the most beautiful hair," he told me. "I could get lost in it, like some wild thicket."

Just then Felix of all people walked by and gave me a raised-eyebrows look. I smiled and waved and hoped he wasn't there to meet Mom, which would be all I needed. With luck, she was too hung over to go out in the sunlight.

We drank our coffee and watched some robins in the flower bed excavate for worms. Bert went past rolling a metal trash can. The lid fell off with a bang and bounced across the patio until Felix scooped it up. Then a car door slammed out in the street, and a little kid went by shrieking at the top of his lungs. When I looked at Jesse, he was white as paste and his hand was shaking so bad he slopped his coffee. He set the cup down crooked in the saucer and looked all around like he was about to either run for it or dive under the table again. I put my hand on his and I could feel the muscles jump.

Felix made it over to our table in about two steps, like some ratty old angel with his bathrobe wings flapping out behind him. He put a hand on Jesse's shoulder, but he was careful to let Jesse see him before he touched him. Jesse slid down in his chair and took a deep breath.

"Pretty noisy day," Felix said.

"Yeah." Jesse reached for his coffee again and knocked it over. "Shit! I'll be right back." He shoved his chair back and went to the coffee bar for napkins. Felix gave me a long look.

"What?" I said.

"This may not be a good idea."

I glared at him. "Not you too."

Felix looked sad and shook his head. "He may have demons you can't imagine."

I thought maybe I could, after dreaming Felix's dreams, but I told Felix, "Then he needs someone to care about him."

Felix said, "Need is a hell of a bad basis for love. I ought to know."

Jesse came back with a handful of napkins. I could see how mad and embarrassed he was for being afraid of a car door and a little kid. Felix helped him mop up the coffee and didn't say anything else. When it was cleaned up, Felix kind of drifted off to the fiction section but I knew he was still watching us. I would really appreciate it if everyone stopped treating me like I was twelve.

"Oh God, I'm sorry," Jesse said. "I really hate it when I do that in front of you."

"It's okay. I don't mind."

"That's because you're my angel. Angel by name, angel by nature. You know, I'd really like to be able to talk without all these people and making an ass of myself. Could we go somewhere? Pack a picnic maybe and have a day in the hills? On a nice day like this?"

Well, that sounded just like heaven to me, but I knew Mom would flip if I even suggested it.

"Um. I'd have to work on that." I bit my thumbnail.

Jesse smiled. "Next weekend? Saturday?"

He looked so hopeful. Somebody has to care about him. He deserves someone to love him. He's only four years older than I am. Ben's six years older than Mom.

"Saturday," I said.

———

On Saturday, I called Jesse and told him to meet me in the park. I told Ben I was going out with Lily and made Lily swear not to rat me out. I've never lied to Ben or Mom about anything important like that before, but I also just caught Mom sneaking out of Ben's bedroom with her dress on inside out. If Mom and Ben can act like that, they don't get to tell me what to do.

Jesse met me with his mom's car. He had a picnic basket covered with a red and white cloth in the back seat.

"Where are we going?" I asked, but he just smiled and said, "I'm going to show you something special."

He turned the car up Highway 33, and after about a mile we pulled onto a dirt road, bumped along it for a while, and parked at the end where a creek comes down the hill. A trail led off from there through the crackling brush, with its dusty clumps of sage and Matilija poppies and outcrops of huge, pale stones.

I got out of the car a little suspiciously. "Are there snakes up here?"

"They buzz," Jesse said. "Anyway, they can bite me." He shook his artificial foot at imaginary snakes. "I want to show you this thing." He hefted the picnic basket and started up the trail.

"What?"

"You'll see," he said mysteriously.

I followed him through the scrub and up a slope of sandy soil and those white stones that look like huge slabs of bone.

Jesse put his good foot on the slope and pulled himself up by a manzanita bush, dragging the picnic basket with him. I scrambled after him. A grasshopper zinged by my head and I ducked, feeling my hair to be sure it hadn't landed in it.

Jesse laughed. "Come on. Up here."

I went up the rest of the way, onto a flat space against the hillside. A rock overhang made a little shelter and Jesse put the picnic basket under it. I ducked in beside him and he pointed at the ceiling.

"Look up there."

I craned my neck. On the underside of the overhang there was an animal scratched into the stone, with bits of old red-brown paint clinging to its ears and tail. It was curved into a U shape, with round eyes and whiskers. I tipped my neck back farther to stare at it. It looked playful, like it might jump off the rock.

"The Chumash people painted him," Jesse said. "A long time ago."

"Oh, he's wonderful." I was in love with the critter already. I wanted to throw a ball for it. "What is it? A dog? Or a fox?"

"He's an otter. Look how long he is, and look at his paws. There used to be otters in the river here. I found him hiking when I was a little kid. You're the only person I've shown him to. If people find out about him they'll spoil him."

"I won't tell anyone." I liked the idea of having a secret otter with Jesse.

Jesse sat down on the rock floor under the otter and pulled the cloth off the basket. "A bottle of root beer and a loaf of bread," he said. "And thou. Also ham sandwiches and grapes."

I sat down beside him and he twisted the cap off the bottle. "I even brought glasses." He poured root beer into one and handed it to me.

"Elegant."

"I thought I probably shouldn't have been feeding you wine at New Year's."

I rolled my eyes. "My mom's the one who got snockered at the party."

Jesse chuckled. "Give her a break. Teachers deserve to get drunk." He unpacked the sandwiches and handed me one and put the grapes on the cloth. It must have been awkward sitting on the ground like that with his leg, but he didn't seem to care.

I smiled at him. "Shall I peel you a grape?"

"Nah. All the vitamins are in the skin. My mother says so."

"Mine too." I pulled one off its stem. Jesse opened his mouth and I tossed it at him, and he managed to catch it. After he swallowed it, he barked like a seal and clapped his hands and we both broke up laughing. Then we settled down and ate our ham sandwiches while the otter watched us.

Jesse leaned his back against the stone and put his right arm around me while he ate with his left hand. "Man, it's nice up here." He sighed. "Man, *you're* nice. I really need this."

We stayed up there all afternoon, just talking about things, like whether you would be a pioneer on Mars if you had the chance and how the Chumash people caught fish up here and where all the otters went. We kissed some, too, and I think I'm in love. I know I am.

When he took me back, he dropped me at Lily's so I could truthfully say I was coming from there. Lily drove me home. She didn't exactly say she didn't approve, but I can tell she's dubious about it, even though she gave Jesse a hug before he left.

"Ange, are you sure about this?"

"Not you, too?"

"No, I just want you to be happy."

"I am happy."

She sighed. "And preferably not get me in trouble."

Um. Yes. That's an issue. I'll have to think of something else. I promised her I would.

———

On Monday there was a drawing of an otter in my locker. He has a fish in his mouth and little hearts coming up from his head like thought balloons. I still haven't figured out a good way to meet Jesse without making Lily lie for me, but I will. And in the meantime, there's lunch and art class.

When we sat down at the lunch table, Lily looked at both of us and said, "If you make gooey faces at each other just once, I'm out of here."

"Can't," Jesse said. "We're strictly on the down-low."

"I hope so."

"We are innocently hanging the winter art show this afternoon," I said. "In full view of the authorities."

Everybody in the class is supposed to pick two of their best pieces from last semester to show off at the PTA meeting. I picked my still life and a picture of the Todal asleep, which is the only time he holds still. Jesse picked his self-portrait, which really is good, if depressing, and a picture of his little sister. I wish I could draw faces like that. My people always look as if they were sewn together in somebody's laboratory. My self-portrait is terrible. There's something about the eyes that just doesn't line up.

We hung everything in the cafeteria, which becomes the Multipurpose Room as soon as the tables are stacked and the spaghetti is wiped off the walls. Nobody's really settled into school yet after winter vacation, so everyone was running around being silly and dancing on the stacks of tables.

"Man, they're like gerbils," Jesse said.

"Spoken from your position as Eldest and Wisest," I said.

"Eldest, maybe." He shook his head. "Not so wise. Some days I feel like I have it all pegged, you know. All the answers. Then the next day it all looks screwy again. My dad thinks I need to go to church."

I pointed to a spot on the corkboard for a picture hanger. "Do you?"

"I don't know." He punched the hanger in and tugged on it a bit to see if it was tight. "I tried it once, but I couldn't concentrate. Here, hang up your monster dog."

I hung the Todal up and straightened him. "To be honest, I've never had any big questions answered in church."

"But you go. You seem really religious."

"Um. My mom makes me go. And my grandmother would be sad if I didn't. And I do like it. It's peaceful. That part might be good."

"My dad said I just need to hand it all to God. I told him I'd tried and God dropped it."

I laughed. "Maybe God hasn't had the right training."

Jesse punched another hanger in and we hung up my still life. "That's pretty."

"Jesse, Felix says there's a guy who was in Afghanistan in the group he goes to at the VA."

"Yeah, he told me."

"I'm not trying to be a psychologist, because I'm not, but I have to wonder if you might figure out more there than in church."

"That's what my mom said when my dad got going about God. I'll think about it."

I guess he really is, because the next day there was a picture in my locker of the otter on a psychiatrist's couch. The psychiatrist is a fish.

Jesse really seems happier lately, and I like the idea that I have something to do with that. It would be nice if I didn't have to act like being his girlfriend is my secret identity. At least there's a pep rally on Friday, where we can just happen to meet up. Ordinarily I would rather watch grass grow than go to a pep rally, but right now it's our best option.

15

I'm worried about Jesse. I thought everything was great, but then he met me at the rally and looked like someone who'd stuck his finger in a light socket. "I hate this," was the first thing he said to me.

"It's pretty lame," I agreed.

"People jumping around shrieking like fools." He looked disgusted.

"Well, that's what they came here for," I said. The cheerleaders were building a fire in a metal tub in the middle of the parking lot. When they lit it, it went up with a whoosh and Jesse closed his eyes.

I put my arm around him. "You want to go somewhere else?"

"Yeah." He nodded with his eyes half closed. "I can't take this. I'm sorry I'm such a drag."

I took his hand and we started over to the benches by the cafeteria.

"Is it the fire that bothers you?" I said before I thought about it. I guess I should have known not to ask that, but he'd been fine when we talked about the VA.

He jerked his hand away and glared at me the way he did last fall about the peace sticker. His eyes were wide open now, and he looked like he was actually going to hit me. His fists balled up. "Leave me the fuck alone! Quit trying to take care of me!"

"I'm not!"

"Yes, you are. You think the poor headcase needs babysitting. *Is it the fire that bothers you?*" He made his voice a babyish singsong. "*Come on, Jesse, share your feelings with Mommy.*"

That made me mad. "You're the one who said you'd think about me when things got crazy. You're the one who said you'd think about going to the VA group. *I* didn't say that. You said it. So what do you expect?"

"I expect to be able to decide for myself!" Now Jesse was shouting. Even people by the fire had turned around to look at us. "Don't play these games with me! I don't need you! You aren't my mother and you aren't my shrink!"

"Well, I don't want to be either one," I said. "Will you quit yelling?"

"No! I'm yelling because you don't listen to me!"

"Everybody's looking at us!" I hissed.

"Why should I care?"

That was when I burst into tears. Not too mature, but about forty people were staring at us now and Jesse was going off like a rocket, shouting at me. "Because you're humiliating me," I said, low enough that he could hear but nobody else could. "I do *not* deserve this."

He stopped shouting then. I could see his whole body shake, and then just suddenly sag as if when the anger vanished there was nothing else left. He didn't say anything for a long time.

I scrubbed my fist across my face. Now that he wasn't shouting, people had quit looking at us. I sniffled.

He put his hands on my shoulders. "You're right. You don't deserve this. I'm an evil asshole. I'm sorry."

"When you get so mad, it scares me," I said.

"I know. I won't do that any more. I promise." Jesse leaned his head against mine so our foreheads were touching. We stood that way for a while, and I could feel him trying to get a grip on himself. Then he straightened up and pulled me to the bench, and sat down with his arm around me.

"There *was* a fire," he said.

I waited.

"I'm like old Char Man. Still trying to make it come out different." He laughed, but it wasn't really a laugh. "Stupid, really."

I took a chance and said, "What happened?"

I thought for a minute that he wasn't going to tell me. Then he said, "When I lost this." He wiggled his fake foot.

"There were three of us." His voice sounded like he was forcing the words out. "I'm the only one that made it. The sergeant was a stand-up guy, not like some. We mattered to him; he took care of us, best he could. When it went down, I got thrown clear. But the Humvee was on fire and I could see him in there, and I couldn't move. That's the last I remember, him in that burning Humvee. I guess I woke up in the hospital, but I knew they didn't make it."

I don't know what you say to something like that. Finally, I said, "I'm sorry." There wasn't anything else that would make any sense.

Jesse stood up. "Now you know. Let's get the hell away from those idiots."

I stood too, and we wandered off until the shadows didn't flicker anymore. We stretched out in the grass behind the rock wall above the soccer field. The moon was up, almost full, and the noise of the pep rally was just a sound like frogs in the distance.

Jesse let out a long breath. "I'm sorry I was a shit."

"Quit apologizing." I'd been upset, but now that he was sorry, I couldn't help wanting him not to feel so bad. I leaned against his shoulder and he kissed the top of my head. I tipped my face up to his.

In a minute I could feel his hands under my sweater. Part of me really wanted to let him go on, and the other part felt like I was on a seesaw. It was just too much. That's the part that rolled over and said, "No, don't."

"Angie—"

"I'm just not ready for this." I sat up and wrapped my arms around my knees.

"Goddammit." He sounded angry, but then I saw he was crying. He scrubbed a hand across his face. "I'm such a freak. No one will ever love me."

"You aren't a freak. And I do love you. It's just going a little too fast."

"Do you promise me?" His face had that intent look he gets, like someone whose skin is on too tight. "Do you promise me that you love me?"

"Ye-es." I stumbled over it a little. I've never told a boy that before.

"Because I need you to *promise*. You don't sound like you mean it."

"You just said you didn't need me!" I blurted out. I was sorry as soon as I'd said it, but it had hurt my feelings and I wasn't quite over it.

His face tightened up again. "So now you're going to hold that against me?"

I stood up. "No. But I need to go home." I could tell he was getting mad again, although it was my fault this time.

"Running away?"

"I told Ben I'd be back by ten."

"Fine!" Jesse didn't stand up. It was clear he wasn't going to walk me back, so I walked home by myself.

Then I climbed in bed and cried until I went to sleep.

————

And now I have a real problem, because somebody saw us and told Mom. Actually I expect somebody told somebody who told somebody else, who was overheard by a teacher, who told Mom. She didn't seem too clear on the details, but she was extremely clear on not liking it. She actually came over to Ben's tonight and they sat me down together. *Parents Reunite to Save Headstrong Daughter*. Not. They sat on opposite ends of the sofa as if there was an alligator between them.

"Mom. He just leaves drawings in my locker. I'm not eloping with him!" That got me a look that said I'd better watch it.

Ben said, "That's not fair," coming to Mom's defense.

Mom said, "I would prefer you not to make the mistakes I made." She looked at Ben. "Any of them."

"I haven't gotten married once yet!" I snapped, which I knew was going too far.

Mom stood up. "I do not want you hanging around with a boy who's nineteen. And you can just cool the love notes in the locker, too. This is the end of this discussion." She went out the front door and I heard her car start up.

"Angela, that was mean," Ben said.

"Why are you standing up for her?" Now *I* was mad. "She wants to *divorce* you!" I stomped off to my room and slammed the door. And I hate having to lie to Mom and Ben. It makes my stomach feel crawly. If they'd just be reasonable, I wouldn't have to.

I don't know how to be around Jesse now. I must be doing something wrong, or this wouldn't keep happening. I thought maybe Felix would know, so I went to see him and took him some coffee for his coffee pot. He was in the garden. I made him promise not to tell Mom anything.

He didn't like that. "I'm not so sure about this, Ange."

"I've always talked to you," I pointed out. "You never told anyone before." If he was going to be St. Felix, he couldn't argue with that.

"This might be special circumstances."

"Fine. Then I won't talk to you, either."

He sighed and said, "Well, step into my office." We went down to the basement and he put his coffee on a shelf. He'd unpacked the nativity we use in the kindergarten room and arranged the Virgin and her baby on the shelf too, beside a glass of lavender sprigs and a candle from the chapel.

I sat on the bottom step. "It's Jesse."

"Can I say I'm not surprised?"

"No."

He fiddled with the lavender and the Virgin, making her a little crown, while I told him what happened at the pep rally. I said, "I don't know how to *be* with him. I probably have too many opinions, but it's not fair of him to tell me he needs me and then treat me like that."

"It's not fair of him to tell you he needs you," Felix said.

"Don't people who love each other need each other?"

He didn't answer that. He said, "You're fifteen."

"That does not mean I'm not capable of loving some-one," I said back.

He turned around and gave me a long look. Then he said, "Oh, shit. I guess it doesn't." He looked up at the ceiling. "That was really unfair. You hear me?"

"Who are you talking to?"

"God. Or the angels. Whoever's in charge of these things."

"I thought that was Cupid." I grinned at him, trying to lighten things up.

"Cupid's a fly-by-night. He's the one that gives people crushes on their gym teacher. Which would be a better bet for you right now. Listen, you may love him, but Jesse doesn't have good brakes. Believe me, I know. And you've got a *right* to opinions."

"He's not always like that," I said. "He's really sweet. And when he gets upset, if I let him calm down, then he's fine."

"And you want a boyfriend you have to walk on egg-shells with?"

"It's not his fault."

"How does that make it different?" Felix said.

"*Because* it's not his fault." I could see what he meant, but it *does* make it different.

"So you're going to give up the right to speak your mind because it's not Jesse's fault if it upsets him and he acts like a jerk?" Felix crossed his arms over his robe and raised his eyebrows at me.

I hadn't thought about it that way, but I think, *Yeah*.

Yeah, I am. I'm going to learn to bend to Jesse when he's like that because if I love him, it's all I can do.

I didn't say that to Felix. I said, "Look, I'll think about it, okay? Thanks for listening to me. And thanks for not telling Mom."

"Probably a mistake," he said morosely.

―――――――

I don't know if he meant for him or me, but it wasn't a mistake. I let Jesse alone for a few days, which was hard, but I made myself do it. On Friday I knew it was all right when there a was a drawing in my locker again. This one was the Duchess of Alba, or maybe it was me. She had even more hair than either of us do. It curled up into the sky and made clouds around her head. There was a little figure of a tiny guy at her feet writing *SorrySorrySorrySorry* on the ground with a huge pencil. That made me laugh so much, it was all worth it.

I wish I could find everyone somebody to pair up with—get Mom and Ben back together, find Lily a nice guy, even find a nice girl for Noah Michalski. He's my biology lab partner this semester and has not thrown fetal pig parts at anyone yet, which for Noah is angelic.

The Ben-and-Mom thing is probably the hardest. Jesse says he wishes his parents would split up; they're hardly talking to each other now. I said I would trade him, I just want mine back together. I can't even figure out a way to throw them into each other's company anymore. I'm out of holidays.

On the other hand, Jesse's birthday is in a week. I've been trying to figure out a birthday present, but I can't ask Mom's advice, obviously, and I've been dodging Felix after the last time. I've finally decided *I'll* take *Jesse* to see the otter. I'll pack us a fancy picnic and a pillow for his leg and something silly like a book of poetry to read to each other. Jesse will have to drive, but Lily says she'll cover for me one more time as her birthday present to him, which is really nice of her.

———————

I bought chocolate-covered espresso beans, which I know Jesse loves, and pomegranate soda just to be exotic, and crusty rolls from the bakery, and three kinds of cheese and sliced meat, and tiny seedless tangerines. For dessert I bought a chocolate torte. I packed it all in a wicker basket I found in some of Mom's stuff that's still in the closet. I couldn't find a book of poetry. Everything on Mom's shelves was either so obscure I didn't know what it was talking about, or else about death and suicide. Or *by* people who committed suicide. There was also one volume of love poems that I would be too embarrassed to read. So I gave up on the poetry idea and bought silly hats at the thrift shop instead—a mini-sombrero for him and a vintage felt hat with a little net veil for me. I told Jesse he had to pick me at Lily's house, and I was very mysterious about it, just to make him curious.

When he rolled up, I hurried out before Lily's mom could notice who I was leaving with and stuffed my basket in the car. I hopped into the front seat.

"Where to, Duchess?" He smiled at me, but he was looking kind of grim.

"Off to see the otter," I said. I didn't ask about the grim look, I just told him, "I have provisions and happy birthday otter-viewing hats in the basket."

Which was apparently the right thing to do, because he let out a long breath and said, "You are the most. Thank you. I needed to get away. I had a horrible morning."

I waited.

"I blew up at Mom," he said. "I lost it. She was ragging on Dad again for letting me enlist, but enlisting was *my* decision. I started shouting, and now my head hurts like hell and I scared Michael and Sarah."

"Wow," I said. "Not a great birthday."

"It'll be all right now," he said.

And it wasn't. It so wasn't.

It started out okay. It was a beautiful day, warm enough to leave my jacket in the car. We scrambled up the slope and I unpacked the picnic and the hats. Jesse cracked up at his. He opened a pomegranate soda and dribbled a little on the rock floor. "For the otter," he said. "And the gods of the place."

I gave the otter a few drops of soda, too. It really is a magical place. I wish I could have lived here when there were otters in the river. After we ate, we cuddled up to watch the sun turn the afternoon sky pink. He gave me a little squeeze and I melted into him, and we slid down onto the stone floor.

Maybe I didn't really think things through, going up there alone with Jesse after what had happened at the pep rally. But it felt so good at first, like he was somebody who belonged to me and everything was happening like it was supposed to, and the otter gave us his blessing.

"Goya painted his duchess naked, too," he whispered to me. "That's the one I really think of when I look at you. I want to paint you that way some day. All your beautiful skin."

He'd moved until he was on top of me, and I felt his fingers sliding down the zipper on my jeans. That was when Felix's dream came back into my head, the one about the girl in the bar. First I was me, then I was Felix. Then for a second I knew what it felt like to be that girl, too. And I knew I didn't want to be that girl and I had to make him stop.

Only I couldn't.

I put my hand over his. "Jesse, I'm not ready for this."

"You promised you love me," he said.

"I do love you, but I just can't."

"It's that Michalski kid, isn't it?" His face was crazy-intent now, like rubber bands were holding everything together.

"No! Don't be stupid!"

"I'm not stupid!" His fingers dug into my arm. "I see him talking to you all the time!"

"His locker's next to mine!" I pushed back at him, but he didn't let go. He kissed me and pressed his mouth on mine so hard that it hurt.

I wiggled harder but Jesse still didn't let go. I tried twisting my head away but he didn't stop. "Let me up!" I was starting to panic.

"Duchess..." He buried his face in my hair and I could feel his hands inside my jeans.

"No! Jesse, don't!"

"I love you." His voice sounded slurred, and stubborn. "I need you. You promised me."

"Let me go!"

His hand pushed me down onto the stone, hard. I was scared and mad at the same time. I turned my head and bit him. I could feel my teeth break the skin on his hand.

"Ow! Goddammit!"

He pulled back just a little and I brought my knee up. I guess it must have hurt some, because he half rolled off me. I jumped up before he could grab me again and slid down the slope to the trail, holding my unzipped jeans up with one hand.

"Angie, wait!"

I could hear him coming after me so I ran, zipping my jeans as I went. I knew I could outrun him with his bad leg.

"Angie! Please! I'm sorry!"

I kept going, past the car and out to the highway.

Highway 33 is a winding two-lane with a dirt shoulder, and I walked along it until I got my breath back. I felt safer out there. There was traffic coming along at a fairly steady rate.

After a couple of minutes I heard a car slow down behind me. It was Jesse, with the passenger window down.

"Angie, I'm sorry. Come on back, baby. I'm sorry."

He sounded so miserable, I felt sorry for him. But I kept walking. "No way."

"Please, baby." Cars behind him were starting to honk. I think he was crying. "You can't walk all the way back."

"I'm going to."

He kept following me, backing up traffic, but I wouldn't stop.

Finally he said, "Then walk!" and threw my jacket out the window at me. He turned his head around to look at the cars behind him. "And fuck you!" He stuck his hand out the driver's window and gave them all the finger. Then he hit the gas and the car rocketed off, screeching around the next bend.

No one offered me a ride, not that I would have taken it. They probably thought I was crazy, too. I walked all the way home. It was three miles, and I was still freaked out and mad and miserable by the time I got there. Ben wasn't around. I slunk into my bedroom and called Lily.

"Oh, Ange," she said when I told her. "I did wonder if he might want to go farther than you would, but I didn't think he was dumb enough to do anything like that."

I sniffled. "I really don't think he would have quit. And

the awful thing is that I do love him, and I really think he loves me."

"I think he does, too," Lily said. "In fact, he told me so."

I started to cry.

Lily hung on until I quit bawling. She's patient. And she promised to go up there with me and collect everything we'd left. I can't leave the otter's cave full of stupid hats and garbage.

"Please don't say anything to Jesse," I said before we hung up. "Or anyone else. I can handle this."

I could tell she doesn't think that's a good idea, but I absolutely can't tell Mom or Ben because they will call the police or something and I can't bear to do that to him.

16

And then, just to top it off, I took the Todal for a walk on Sunday after church so I could think and bumped right into Jesse's mother at the Stop-In. I'd told the Todal to sit and went inside looking for a chocolate fix, and there she was, buying a quart of milk.

"Angela! How nice to see you." She waved the milk at me. "We're always out of *something* if it's Sunday. You looked just lovely New Year's Eve. I've wanted to tell you."

"Um, thanks, Mrs. Francis." I swiveled my head around to see if Jesse was with her, and he wasn't, thank God.

"How's school?"

"It was nice being on vacation. Kind of hard to go back."

"Oh, I expect so. I think Jesse was glad to go back,

though. It's hard for him to be idle." The clerk bagged her milk and handed it to her, and she smiled at me. "I'm very glad Jesse has made friends with you. It's been difficult for him, and having someone like you is such a blessing."

"We don't really see each other at school much," I said. "Except for art. I'm just a sophomore." What happened to her worrying about him hanging out with younger kids?

"When you're such good friends, maybe that age gap doesn't matter so much," Mrs. Francis said, like she was convincing herself. "Jesse has always followed his own path, from the time he was little. I've stopped worrying about that, so don't you worry about it." She patted my shoulder. "I'm just glad he has you. I think he's having a bad day today, though. Maybe you could call him."

"Um, sure." *No!*

She offered me a ride home, but fortunately I had the Todal with me.

———

After obsessing about it all day, I went back to St. Thomas's. I've got nobody I can talk to about all this. So if Felix thinks coming alive gets him off the hook, he has another think coming.

He was in his basement. He looked up when he saw me clumping down the stairs. "Angela! I thought you'd given me the brush-off."

"I need to talk to someone. Where is my statue?"

He'd been sewing a button on a shirt, and he put it

down and scooted over to make room for me next to his space heater. It was chilly in the basement, and the space heater made a little puddle of hot air.

"I don't know," he said.

"Felix—"

He shook his head and looked sad. "No, I really don't. I think it used to be me, or I used to be it. That's what it seemed like. But I'm not sure."

He was wearing the bathrobe again. "Have you been to see a psychiatrist? Ever?"

"Oh, yeah. Lots. But I hate the medication, you know? It makes me feel like I'm half there."

"You weren't there at all, before," I said. "But at least I could talk to you. I mean, to the statue."

"Do you miss that? You can't talk to your mom?"

"I mostly talked to you *about* my mom."

"I'm sorry."

"That's not good enough. My mom got drunk New Year's Eve and hooked up with Ben! I saw her sneak out of the house with her underwear in her hand!"

"I didn't think she was over him," Felix said.

"It's not fair!" I could feel my eyes starting to sting. "I asked Ben if they were getting back together and he said *no*. How can they do that?" I sniffled. Tears were starting to run down my face, and I just let them. Everything was so awful.

Felix put his arm around my shoulders, the way Mom used to when somebody had teased me. "Sex is a very mysterious thing," he said, like he was thinking it over. "I've never understood it well myself. They may not, either."

"I don't understand anybody!" I said. I was crying now, hiccupping and really bawling.

Felix patted me and I put my head on his shoulder, sniffling into his bathrobe. It was warm from the heater and smelled like cigarette smoke. The heater was making little pinging noises and it was really nice to have someone hug me who wasn't trying to kiss me or stick his hand in my clothes.

"And I haven't even told you the worst thing!" The thing I really need to tell someone.

"Yeah?"

"It's Jesse."

He sighed.

"You were right. I can't handle this."

"What happened?"

"I thought I could make it all be okay if I just didn't upset him, you know? And it was fine for a while. He was doing really well."

"Until?"

I told Felix all about the otter's cave and the picnic, even the silly hats. "It seemed like such a great idea for his birthday. To start with." I sniffled because I'd liked the otter so much and Jesse had spoiled it.

"To start with, and not later?"

The heater made another pinging noise and shot sparks out of its back. Then the whole basement went dark.

"Oh, crap."

"What happened?" I asked.

"It blew the fuse. I can go fix it if you want."

"No, it doesn't matter." I didn't want him to leave.

"It'll get cold."

"You can fix it when it gets cold." I wanted to tell him about Jesse. That was spooking me more than the dark.

"Okay. So what happened later?"

"We made out."

"What kind of making out?"

I was glad the lights were out. It was easier to talk about it in the dark. "Kind of extensive making out. And he wouldn't stop."

"I don't like that 'wouldn't stop' part," Felix said.

"I didn't either. And I got really scared and I bit him and made him let me go, and I ran off and walked home. He followed me in the car and made a scene and backed up traffic."

Felix gave a kind of chuckle. "You bit him, huh? You're going to be just fine." He chuckled again. "It feels awful now, but you're going to be just fine."

I thought about how I knew how that bar girl in his dream had felt, and how I hadn't wanted to be her. I didn't say it though. He was only about Jesse's age then. But the dream suddenly made more sense to me. All of Felix's other dreams are things he feels guilty about. I bet he feels guilty about that one, too.

"And I saw Jesse's mom in the Stop-In this morning. She said she was so glad Jesse had me for a friend, but I could tell she meant girlfriend. She thinks it's great."

"I expect she's pretty desperate." Felix was quiet for a

long time then, just holding me snuggled up against him where I felt safe. "I assume you know it would be a good idea to not hang out with him alone anymore," he said finally.

"I won't just abandon him. I'm not going to be like Mom."

"You aren't abandoning him."

I sniffled again. "I really care about him. But now he scares me. I hate that."

"Go ahead and feel bad for him. I feel bad for him, too. You can even care about him. But pay attention to your gut instincts, okay? They're probably more reliable than your emotions."

"I really wanted to help him."

"Fix him up?" I could hear Felix smiling in the dark.

"He seemed better when he was with me," I said.

"Until he wasn't," Felix said. "Ange, if anyone is going to fix Jesse, it will have to be Jesse."

"I'm afraid he'll be worse after this. That I made him worse."

"He may be worse, but it won't be your fault. Or your responsibility."

I felt a little better, even if I'm getting counseling from a crazy homeless guy who lives in a basement. I think the only person Felix can't figure out is himself.

Then we heard voices and people bumbling around at the top of the stairs. Felix started to get up. "Better fix that fuse."

Before I could move to let him stand up, someone

shone a flashlight down the stairs right in our eyes. I heard a kind of shriek and a gasp.

"It's okay," I said. "It's just us."

Felix stood and felt his way to the fuse box and the lights came on in a minute. He must have to do it all the time if he runs that heater much.

It was Altar Society ladies at the top of the stairs, Mrs. Beale and Mrs. Rausch. They're friends of Wuffie's.

"Angela!" Mrs. Beale said. She kept the flashlight trained on Felix as if it was a gun. "Call the police!" she said over her shoulder to Mrs. Rausch.

17

I finally persuaded them not to call the police, but I don't think I really convinced them that Felix wasn't molesting me or doing something else awful. I told them that Father Weatherford knew he was living here, that Felix was doing the gardening. Felix just stood there in his bathrobe, looking sad.

It's not fair. Now they want to throw him out. They've all seen him in the garden, and at the Posadas parade, and even said how nice everything is looking, but now they've decided he's dangerous. I know it's because of me, and nobody will listen to me. I went to talk to Father Weatherford, and he acted like he was going to pat me on the head and gave me some story about insurance liabilities that is totally smoke and mirrors. I guess the church is pretty sensitive about people molesting people, but that was priests. I didn't say that to Father Weatherford. I said it to Ben, and he laughed and said, "'Whatever a man prays for, he prays for a miracle. Every prayer reduces itself to this: Great God, grant that twice two be not four.'"

I said, "What?" and he said that's what Ivan Turgenev, who was some Russian writer, had to say about prayer. Helpful.

I thought maybe Wuffie could do something, but she says the Altar Society won't listen to her and maybe it's a better idea if Felix sleeps at the Rescue Mission or some shelter. And this is the man who bathes her dog when it has fits! And he doesn't want to sleep at the Rescue Mission, where they try to convert him. He likes the church.

So now he's sleeping under a tree in the park.

I took him a better sleeping bag and one of Ben's sweaters and some socks. Ben's socks. I didn't ask and it serves him right.

Felix says he asked Father Weatherford if it was still okay if he came around and took care of the garden during the day. I think Felix needs that garden.

My whole life is like one of those tables with a wobbly leg. You prop up one side and the other side gets off kilter and slides your soup into your lap. Jesse wasn't in school today, which was a relief, but I keep wondering what he's doing, if he's sitting in his room drawing mazes again. I just want everybody back where they belong: Felix in his basement and Mom home with Ben. Really home, not hooking up with him, which I don't think she would do if she intended to come back and live with him.

She called before I went to school this morning to say she wanted to have a little chat with me after school. She probably wants to tell me the divorce is final and she's enrolled me in a convent while she goes to Paris to write poetry.

Oh God. The world sucks. The world totally sucks. Wuffie picked me up after school instead of Mom and took me to her house. I don't know whether Mom had planned to explain New Year's Eve or yell at me some more about Jesse, but now she's forgotten all about it. She's in bed at four in the afternoon, crying. Darren Hardison, who was in her English class when I was little and always called me Punkin, is dead.

He was killed in Afghanistan last night. She just found out. He used to come back to see her after high school, and when he was at college, he'd send her funny cards and strange news clippings. Once he sent her one about a man who drove all the way to San Diego on a riding lawnmower.

Mom couldn't stop crying. She was crying so hard she was choking. Her face was red and she sounded like a dog howling. I've never heard anyone cry like that.

Finally she stopped. She sniffled and wiped her face with the sheet and held her arms out to me. I hugged her, remembering Darren, how he used to slip me candy bars. She sniffed again and I handed her a tissue from the dresser. She blew her nose and leaned her head against my shoulder.

"But why are you in bed?" All her old stuffed animals were piled around her, including First Husband's rabbit.

"I don't know what else to do. I just want to pull the covers over my head and stay here." Her voice sounded like somebody else. I've never seen Mom like this. The Mom I'm used to would organize an anti-war march and call her congressman.

"Why don't you come home?"

She didn't answer that. She said, "I've been trying to say a rosary for him, but I keep ending up just crying."

I told her I thought the Virgin could figure out what she meant, and she said, "Yeah," kind of sadly.

I thought about the time Darren sent Mom flowers when he got an A on his college Shakespeare final because he remembered something she'd taught him, and I felt sad to my bones. He was her favorite and he was always nice to me. He recognized I was *there*. Usually big kids don't recognize little kids are there.

"When is the funeral?" I asked her.

"I don't know," she said. She closed her fist around the rabbit's ears and shut her eyes. "It doesn't matter. Funerals don't bring them back."

———

Now all I can think about is what the Chumash thought about the dead going away over the water and how you can hear the doors of the underworld bang shut after them. I keep seeing all the dead boys—and girls too—walking across the water like Jesus to the Underworld. The door sounds like it's metal, like prison doors closing. I wonder if Jesse knew Darren. I'm scared to ask. Jesse came to school today and when I opened my locker, about a hundred little drawings fell out. They were all mazes. Some of them had his face in the middle and some of them had mine. I scooped them up and stuffed them in the trash, and then pulled them out again for fear someone would see them.

Darren's obituary was in the paper this morning and everybody at school is talking about it.

In English, Mrs. Larsen told us to write what we felt about loss and death, so I wrote a poem for Darren.

The Path to the Underworld

leads across grey swells.
Beyond the seal rocks off Anacapa Island
the dead travel light of foot.
You can hear the doors bang shut
behind them, stone on stone
reverberating inside what is left:
feathers, bones, flame, sand.

It's like something Mom would do. Mom, on the other hand, called in sick this morning and is still in bed. I talked to Wuffie on the phone and Wuffie says she won't get up. I told Ben before I left for school, thinking maybe he'd go over there, and he just said, "She'll get up when she wants to."

I saw Jesse at lunch. He was hunched over his tray, by himself. He didn't look up and I was kind of relieved. I sat down with Lily at a different table.

"Don't go near Jesse," she said.

"Huh?" I wasn't going to if I could help it, but still.

"I asked him if he knew Darren Hardison and he said to go fuck myself." She didn't look insulted. I guess you understand things when your mom's a shrink. Sometimes I think I could tell Lily I fantasize I'm a blue baboon and she would just say "uh huh" and go on eating her sprout sandwich. I wish I was like that.

"I'm scared," I said. "Wuffie says to pray, but I don't know what to pray for. Comfort, I guess. Wars to stop. But I don't think God's even listening."

"My dad says, give a man a fish and you'll feed him for a day. Give him a religion and he'll starve to death while praying for a fish," Lily said. Considering that her folks lived in a monastery, they're pretty cynical about organized religion. Lily says the monastery wasn't organized.

I don't want a fish. I want two and two to be not four, and Darren Hardison not to be dead. I want Jesse to be okay.

———

Jesse went home after lunch. He didn't come to art class.

After school I went to see Felix in the park. There's a live oak with a huge low limb that sticks straight out, about four feet off the ground, at the place where the park runs into the scrub brush near the old railroad tracks. He's made a little cave under it, out of a tarp. When the city notices him, they'll probably make him move too. I keep telling him how sorry I am about the church throwing him out, and he keeps saying it's not my fault. But I feel like it is.

"Sit down. Have a pomegranate. Your grandmother gave me some." He handed me one and I dug my fingernails into the skin. He's swept all the oak leaves away from in front of his tree, and he has a hibachi set up on the dirt, with a dishpan to wash things in.

"You're like a mobile home," I said, smiling. He even has art—there are pictures cut out of magazines pinned to the back wall of the tarp: a close-up of a red and green frog and a bouquet of poppies.

"It's hard to find a good hobo jungle anymore," he said. "Gotta make your own. I miss my nice coffeemaker, though."

I picked seeds out of the pomegranate, watching my fingers turn purpley-red, and told him about Darren Hardison and Mom lying in bed crying.

"It's tough on her, having all those kids," he said.

"They aren't hers," I said.

"Yeah, they are."

And he's right. Darren Hardison might as well have been. "Is that how you felt about the soldiers you were with in the army?" I asked. "Like you wanted to save them all?"

"You can't save people."

"Sometimes you can. You did."

"Never. You can help. But they save themselves or they don't. I've told you that."

That sentence made me feel like I couldn't breathe. I put the pomegranate down. "You just … watch?" I said. "*Everyone?*"

"Yeah. You just watch."

I don't think I am going to be able to stand life if that's true. I saw a cat get hit by a car once. I could see the car coming and the cat in the street, and I screamed at it to get out of the way but it didn't. The car kept coming, and when it hit the cat, it spun it around on its back. They didn't even stop. I picked up the cat and I made Mom drive us to the vet with it, but it was dead by the time we got there. I wouldn't believe it was dead. I held it in my lap, wrapped up in a towel, all the way to the vet and I was sure he would save it.

I stared at the pomegranate juice on my fingers and remembered how the cat's blood had soaked my jeans. Is it going to be like that with people? Does God really just let things randomly happen? Surely he can't *want* some of the things that happen to be that way. Wars and little kids dying, and Darren being dead? Why would God want that? So it must be random.

It's not as if that never occurred to me before. But I never thought about *my* life being random. About things happening to *me* being random. About somebody I love just dying. About somebody I love coming to pieces. How do people live with that? Once something like that happens to you, how do you go on living your normal life and not be paralyzed with terror that something else is going to drop out of the sky on you? That the next car that comes by will spin you around in the road like that cat?

21

Ben was waiting for me when I got home, with some more great news. Father Weatherford called him and said I have to see a counselor about "what happened in the basement."

"What?" I said.

Ben looked uncomfortable. "He's worried about Felix."

"Well, he ought to be," I said. "He hasn't got any place to live, thanks to those busybodies."

"He didn't mean that, I'm afraid," Ben said. "He means he's concerned that Felix may have hurt you in some way."

He was watching me carefully to see what I did. I could tell. I nearly lost it. "That is the stupidest thing I ever heard!" I was almost shrieking. "Do they think I'm a moron? Do they think he's some kind of child molester? They don't know shit!"

"And you do?"

I tried to get a grip. "I know Felix isn't dangerous. To me or anybody else. You ask Mom!" I glared at him.

Ben sighed. "I did. She said the same thing."

"Has she quit crying?"

"No."

I started to cry again, too. "I hate this! I hate everything that's happening! I hate people getting killed, and you and Mom splitting up, and I hate being scared of everything!"

"Oh, honey." Ben looked really sad. "Maybe you can talk to the counselor about that, since Father Weatherford wants you to go see him."

"Him? Him who?"

"I think you can pick. He said the parish would pay for it."

"This is about 'insurance liabilities,' isn't it?" I asked.

"Probably. I expect the church is a little gun-shy, on the whole."

"Fine," I said. "I'll go see Lily's mom. But I cannot believe they want me to see a shrink. And I am not going to see someone who's already decided Felix must have molested me and will try to make me remember stuff that didn't happen! And I'll run up a big bill. Their insurance company can pay *that*."

I especially hate that they're hounding someone who's

been a comfort to me, and telling me to be scared of him, too. I'm already scared of enough stuff.

I told Lily what they're making me do and asked her if it would be weird for her, me seeing her mom, because it occurred to me later that it might be. It would have been an out. But she just said, "No, Mom has pretty good sense." Which doesn't sound like a testimonial, but is a lot more than I can say for my mom. So I have an appointment for Friday.

———

Jesse came to school again yesterday, but he's still acting like there's nobody else in the room with him most of the time. It's freaky. There haven't been any more pictures in my locker. He sits hunched over at lunch, eating his sandwich like somebody's going to take it away from him. He didn't even answer when Mr. Petrillo talked to him in art. Mr. Petrillo just went on to the next person, which was me. We have assigned tables, so I'm still next to Jesse. Jesse was acting like I wasn't there, which was kind of a relief. We're studying the Impressionists, and Mr. Petrillo has us painting a tub full of water lilies, trying to be Monet. Mr. Petrillo looked at my water lilies and said he liked the way I'm handling the light that reflects on the water from the studio skylight. When he went on to the next person, I snuck a look at Jesse.

He was painting a water lily petal, up close, with his

nose practically in the paint. Just painting the same stroke over and over again.

He caught me looking at him and I thought he was going to get mad. But he shook his head, like someone trying to shake water out of his ears, and he suddenly smiled at me and said, "Hey, do you want to go up to Rose Valley tomorrow? We can take your silly dog and hike up to the waterfall."

I stared at him. Rose Valley is a place up in the foothills where people go to camp. There's a waterfall and picnic tables and nothing else. And he thought I'd go *there* with him? After what happened Saturday?

"Yeah," he continued, like nothing had happened with us. "It's so peaceful up there. I saw a roadrunner on the old fire trail once. I need to go someplace where there's just birds and trees, you know. I need to go there with you."

"Jesse—"

"You're not still mad, are you? Just because we had a fight?"

A fight? "That was more than a fight," I hissed at him.

"I thought you loved me!" he snapped. "I love you." He smacked his hand down on the edge of his easel, hard enough to rattle it on its legs, and people turned around to stare at us. I ought to get used to it.

"Anyway, my folks won't let me," I said in a hurry, because I was afraid he'd start yelling. "They think I'm too young to go in cars with boys." Which wasn't strictly true, but would be if they knew it was Jesse.

"You snuck off before, didn't you?" Jesse said.

"I got caught. They grounded me." Also not true, but there's no way I'm going to go up to Rose Valley alone with Jesse.

He stared at me. "Are we going to let that matter?" He shook his head. "Angie, I need you."

The bell rang and I started stuffing things back into my bag. "I've got to go. I've got a doctor's appointment after school."

"Call me when you get back. We need to talk about this."

I took off before he could say anything else and got in Ben's car like bears were after me. Ben must have thought I looked funny because he said, "Are you okay with this, Angelfish? You don't have to go back if you don't want to. Just the once, to keep the rector happy."

"It's okay." I'm probably the only person in Ayala who's never seen a shrink before, anyway. We know people who have a personal therapist, and a group therapist, and a couples therapist, and one for the dog. And in any case, I have to say that Lily's mom is kind of cool. All Lily's friends call her by her first name, Helen, and she has blond hair in a bowl cut and round glasses. She's pretty like Lily but she never seems to pay any attention to what she looks like. Once she had on shoes that didn't match.

"It's nice to see you, Angela," she said, opening the door to her office. "I understand you're here under protest."

"Ben says I don't have to come again if I don't want to," I told her. "But I want to come long enough to run up a huge bill so you can send it to the parish. I'm furious at them." I plopped down on her couch.

"I'm not sure that's entirely ethical."

"It wasn't ethical to kick Felix out of the church basement when I *told* them he hadn't done anything to me."

"And you're quite certain about that?"

"Yes! Do they think I'm so dumb I can't tell what somebody's doing? And what makes them think *they* can tell who's dangerous and who's not? I don't see how anybody can tell that!" Plainly, I can't.

"Well, it's not easy," Helen said. "There are signs we look for. Behavior that's appropriate and behaviors that aren't. And, of course, sometimes we're wrong anyway."

"Well, Felix hasn't done anything that's inappropriate. I *told* them that."

"Do you want a drink?" She waved a hand at a little refrigerator in the corner, under a stack of magazines. "And who exactly is 'they'?"

"Father Weatherford and two Altar Society ladies." I picked a can of mango juice and curled up again on the couch. "And some insurance company moron that's all worried about getting sued."

Helen kind of snorted. She has the funniest laugh. "It's the function of insurance companies to worry about getting sued. They do it for a living."

"Can't you tell them Felix is okay?"

"If I'm convinced he is, I can."

"What do I have to do to convince you? This isn't fair.

People are supposed to be innocent until someone proves they're not, not the other way around!"

"True. But when it comes to the issue of child abuse, people are often not inclined to wait until someone is hurt."

I said, "I. Have. Not. Been. Hurt," and glared at her.

Helen looked like she was trying to decide something. She bit the end of her pencil, which she hadn't been writing with but kept sticking behind her ear and then taking it out again. "There are privacy issues, you understand. Things I can't tell you because they're about other people."

"Uh huh." I wasn't sure where this was going, but I didn't like it. "If you mean you think you know something bad about Felix, but you can't tell me what it is—"

"Calm down. The opposite is equally possible."

"You mean you know something good?" She didn't say anything. "Possibly?"

"Hypothetically speaking—"

I started paying attention. She wasn't going to tell me if I wasn't careful.

Helen said, "Hypothetically speaking," again. "As just as a *for instance*, if a counselor was concerned about a client's relationship with another person, if the counselor wondered if that other person might be destructive or not, and that other person had a counselor too—"

"You might talk to that other counselor," I said. "Pretending that you weren't, of course."

Helen snorted again. "You're quick on the uptake."

"Felix has a counselor at the VA he sees sometimes."

"Does he? Fancy that."

"What did he tell you?"

Helen sighed. "You aren't doing this right."

I remembered Grandma Alice talking about how her husband wrote home during the war, pretending he was telling her some movie plot. "Ben's working on a new film," I said. "There's this homeless guy in it, he's a Vietnam veteran, he used to be a medic and he still worries about the soldiers he couldn't save, and he lives in a church basement and makes friends with this girl."

"Does he?" Helen said. "An interesting approach, Cleversides. I'd like to see that movie. Well, given his background, rather than wanting anything from the girl, I think this character might be more likely to see himself as a rescuer—her protector—don't you?"

"Absolutely," I said.

Helen nodded. "I expect that comes out when he talks to his counselor."

I expect it did, I thought, and I was really grateful for Helen and the counselor at the VA, who were willing to break the rules to keep something awful from happening. To either one of us. So I said, "Thank you." And then, "If we don't say anything about other counselors and stuff like that, is it okay to actually talk about Felix and me?"

"That's what you're here for."

"If you tell them he's okay, and he wouldn't hurt anyone, will they let him move back into the church?"

"I honestly don't know, but I'm going to try to convince them."

We talked some about how people get worked up and

assume that what they expect to happen is what really *is* happening, and they don't want to hear anything that conflicts with that. Like the Altar Society ladies.

"That's what Felix told me," I said. "I don't see how a person can be as smart as he is sometimes and be somebody who's living under a tree."

"The hardest person to impart wisdom to is ourselves," Helen said. I really like Helen.

"Do you think people's trauma, you know, *leaks?*" I asked.

"Leaks?"

"Hypothetically speaking, um, if a person has weird dreams, and they are actually somebody else's dreams, would you say that person was crazy?"

"It's called mutual dreaming," Helen said. "When two people have the same dream. There is actually a good deal of research that's been done on that. Some of it's a bit out-there, but I wouldn't say it's evidence of outright insanity." She smiled at me. "There are some dreams that almost everyone has—like being naked in public. Or having to take an exam you're not prepared for."

"Not those," I said. "And I don't mean just dreaming the same dream."

"Well, maybe you should tell me more."

"And maybe you'll think I ought to be locked up. Okay, look, Felix has these dreams, nightmares really, from Vietnam. Recurring dreams? Of being in the jungle and people getting blown up. And, uh, one about a bar girl."

"I see."

"And now I've started having them. The same dreams. I don't mean I'm just there, I mean I'm *him*. And I told him about them, and he recognized them. They're *his* dreams. In *my* head. Dreams he's had for years, since before I was born."

"Interesting." Helen really did look interested, not like she was about to call the Psych Ward.

"Even the one about the bar girl." I might as well spill it all. "Which was really weird and gross. They had sex. And I was *him*."

"It's certainly a sign of a connection."

"That was too connected."

"I can see how it might have been. Have you told anyone else about these dreams?"

"Just Lily."

"And what did Lily say?" her mom asked. "I have a good deal of respect for Lily's take on things."

"She said now I knew something I didn't know before, about sex."

Helen chuckled. "Lily's a practical girl. In a way, that's true. Generally people don't get to see what it would be like to be the opposite gender. It might give you a certain understanding, later on."

I hadn't thought about it that way. It actually already had given me a certain understanding, which I wasn't going to mention to Helen. But I guess even things you don't want to know can be useful. Although it was still way beyond creepy.

"Has anyone else ever told you about something like

this before?" I asked Helen. Maybe it was common—Leaking Dream Syndrome—and there was some magic medication.

"No. You're the first."

Of course. If anyone is going to develop a weird new psychiatric problem, it will be me.

"I really don't know what's going on," Helen said gently. "But my best advice would be, don't let it frighten you. Sometimes dreams are our heads trying to tell us things, and yours may have just taken an unorthodox route. I read about a man who dreamed he had a tumor in his 'neck brain' and his doctor just laughed at him and said there was no such thing. But he kept having the dream so he went for a scan anyway, and he had developed a tumor in his brain stem, which is the part at the back of the neck. That was a pretty straightforward dream. I don't think yours are trying to tell you anything that simple. But just listen to them. Go along for the ride. Be in the movie, so to speak, and see if you can tell yourself you're dreaming. Then take some notes when you wake up. See if anything of you has crept in, or if it's all still Felix."

"Are you going to write me up as a case study?"

Helen chuckled. "Tempting, but no. But you could be your own science experiment."

I decided I might as well go for broke. "There's one more thing."

Helen waited for me to tell her what it was.

"It's really Felix's thing, but it's ..." I took a deep breath and blurted it out. "He says he's a saint and that God found out he wasn't holy enough and de-sainted him."

Helen raised her eyebrows but she didn't interrupt me. I guess shrinks are trained not to.

I said, "I know that doesn't make sense, but there was a statue of a saint called Felix in the church basement, and I used to talk to it. It was just something safe to tell things to, you know? Then this summer I went down there and the statue was gone and Felix was there, and he knew all the things I'd been talking about. He says he's St. Felix and God sent him back for not being saintly. I know he can't be, he's just been living in the basement and listening to me talk to the statue, but the statue is *gone*. I can't find it. And he does kind of look like it." That sounded even crazier than the dreams. I looked at Helen to see if now I'd gone over the line.

"Is it Felix's delusion that's bothering you?" she asked me. "Or the fact that you can't find the statue?"

"The statue. And I've looked everywhere it could be."

"Well," Helen said, "that might explain the dreams. You've been talking to him all these years. That would open up a psychic connection if anything would."

I stared at her. "You think it's true?"

"I have no idea. That's like asking if angels can dance on a pinhead. In the eighth dimension, maybe they can. Maybe he used to be St. Felix in some other life."

I have to admit that if I were him, what happened in the war would certainly make me want to go back to being that other person instead, the one who never had to kill anyone and lived a peaceful life in a monastery.

"On the other hand," Helen said, "people who've been wounded are vulnerable to anything that explains their pain. If he spent his youth trying to save soldiers who couldn't be saved, he might feel a kinship with a saint who's also being asked to do the impossible. All those prayers for things he can't grant. Does it really matter who he is?"

"I don't know. But I'm only comfortable with the idea of miracles when they happened in 1520."

Helen smiled. "Don't think of it as a miracle. You should read up on what theoretical physicists say about the universe. It all sounds like miracles me."

"So maybe he's both?"

"Could be." She looked at her watch. "Hour's up. You can come back if you want, to talk about it some more, and we'll stick the parish with the bill. But in the meantime, I'll tell them my professional opinion is that they're overreacting and your friend is harmless."

"Thanks. You won't tell them about that part—what I just told you—will you?"

Helen smiled. "It's all conjecture, isn't it?"

———

I don't know whether I'll go back or not. Helen wasn't much help about the St. Felix thing. But on the other hand, it's nice to have someone who's professionally licensed tell you that you're not crazy.

19

While I was waiting for Ben to pick me up, I looked at my cell phone. I had eleven missed calls, all of them from Jesse. I turned the ringer back on and it rang again while I was trying to decide whether I should call him or not.

"You were supposed to call me when you finished with the doctor." He sounded wound up; he was talking really fast. "What kind of doctor was it? Are you okay?"

"Jesse, that is totally not your business." I sat down on the edge of a planter outside Helen's office.

"I worry about you, Angie."

"Well, I'm not dying of anything. And I just this minute got out. You've called me eleven times."

"Well, you didn't call me back."

"Eleven times, three minutes apart."

"It seemed like longer. Sorry. I'm on the phone, for Christ's sake!"

"What?"

"That's my mom. She's been bugging me all day."

"Listen, Jesse, I've got to go. I have homework."

"It's Friday. Are you going to Rose Valley with me tomorrow?"

"My parents aren't going to let me do that."

"I waited all afternoon to talk to you!" Now he sounded mad. "I was supposed to go to the VA and I blew them off for you!"

"Jesse, I told you I can't go. I don't want you to miss appointments for me. That's not good."

"It wasn't important. They think I have something wrong with my head, but they're full of it."

"With your head?"

"From the explosion. The doc's trying to tell me that head injuries don't get diagnosed at first sometimes, and they want me to have a scan and they're full of it."

"Maybe they aren't." Now I was getting worried. "Jesse, go get the scan."

"If I do, will you go to Rose Valley with me?" He sounded crafty.

"I told you, I can't do that." I could see Ben's car coming down the street with the Todal's head sticking out the window.

"Tell them you're going with Reindeer."

"I can't ask her to lie for me again. Listen, I have to go." I wasn't going to have this conversation in front of Ben.

"Do you want me to have that scan for you?"

"I want you to have the scan for *you*! It's *your* head! I have to get off the phone now." I snapped it shut as Ben pulled up. I shoved the Todal into the back seat and got in. He hung his head over my shoulder and drooled.

"Everything okay?" Ben asked.

"Yeah." I sighed. "Helen's going to tell the parish I'm not molested and they ought to let Felix move back, but I bet they won't."

"They may not. Your mom called. She's out of bed and she wants to know if you want to go to Darren Hardison's funeral with her." He looked as exasperated as I felt. Mom had probably been weeping at him on the phone, but she still won't come home.

I called her when we got back. She'd quit crying but she sounded miserable. She said she'd pick me up tomorrow. Then I turned my cell all the way off.

———

I haven't been to that many funerals. Ben had a secretary who used to come to the house and take dictation, a sweet woman I just loved. She died and I went to her funeral. I guess I was ten. The minister talked about how her death was a call for everyone there to come to Jesus, and Ben and Mom sat there and ground their teeth. And a teacher of mine died when I was in first grade. I don't really remember that one at all, except for all the flowers.

I will remember Darren Hardison's funeral as long as I live.

It was in the chapel at the funeral home. There was a funeral home woman in a black suit who showed us where to go, past other rooms with flowers and big shiny coffins on stands.

We signed the guest book by the chapel door. Inside, there were more flowers and an organist was playing something I didn't recognize, generic funeral music. Darren's coffin was in front, draped with a flag. An honor guard of soldiers in their blue dress uniforms and white gloves stood on either side of it. They were absolutely expressionless, and I wondered if they have to do this a lot. I'm not sure I could stand that. But it would be worse, I guess, to be the ones who have to go to somebody's house to tell them. Mom sat beside me with tears running down her face the whole time. Darren's mom sat in the front pew in a black dress, with her head bent over like she had her face in her hands.

The program said, A CELEBRATION OF THE LIFE OF DARREN HARDISON. We sang "Rock of Ages" and "Amazing Grace" and the minister didn't try to tell anyone to come to Jesus or that Darren had given his life for a good cause; he just said that we cannot know the ways of God but must trust that there is purpose in life and be kind to each other. I liked him.

Afterward, the honor guard carried the coffin out and put it in the hearse, and we all got in our cars to follow them to the cemetery. At the cemetery, the soldiers slid the coffin out of the hearse again and put it in a kind of sling that would lower it into the grave. The grave was already dug, waiting for him, and I kept thinking about how he had flown all the way here from Afghanistan in his coffin, dead. I guess it wasn't the same coffin. This one was shiny and expensive-looking, like his mom had wanted him to have the best place to be that she could manage. It gave me claustrophobia just looking at it. The soldiers took the flag off and folded it up into a triangle. They handed it to Darren's mom and she wrapped her arms around it while a motor started up and the coffin swung out over the grave and began to sink down into it. The minister read some prayers from his book, and Mom went up to Darren's mom and put her arm around her. Darren's mother buried her face in Mom's shoulder.

There was an awful thunk, and they started shoveling dirt into the grave, on top of the coffin. I couldn't stand it. I went and sat in our car and cried.

Finally Mom came. She slid into the driver's seat and put her head down on the wheel for a minute. Then she looked at me.

"Oh, baby. You're grieving, aren't you? And I haven't been paying any attention to you." Her hair looked wilder than ever, corkscrewing out in all kinds of strange directions, and her eyes were red.

I wanted to say she sure hadn't, but I didn't have the heart to. It is entirely possible that I am not the center of the universe. I thought about what Felix said about them all being her kids.

I said, "It's okay."

Mom sniffled. "It's not. I've made a mess of everything. It's wonderful how a funeral focuses your attention on things like that."

I didn't know if she meant the divorce, but I thought it might not be a good idea to ask her right now, and anyway I have enough messes of my own to worry about. And I keep thinking about how he used to call me Punkin.

———

Jesse was waiting for me when Mom dropped me off at Ben's—sitting on the front steps, patting his foot and looking at his watch. Mom didn't say anything when she saw him, but I could see Ben through the living room window and it was crystal clear that Ben had him on his radar screen. I guess Mom decided to leave it to Ben, because she just sniffled and said, "Take care of yourself, sweetie," and drove off.

Jesse said, "Where have you been?"

That was just about too much. I said, "I've been at a funeral," and started to push past him.

He stood up fast and grabbed my arm.

Before I could say anything, Ben was through the front door. "What the hell do you think you're doing?"

Jesse let go of me. I said, "Ben, go away."

"Like hell I will!"

Jesse said, "I have to talk to Angela."

Ben gave him a really evil look. "No one manhandles my daughter."

"I was just trying to talk to her, sir."

Neither one of them was paying any attention to me.

"Hey!" I said. They quit glaring at each other and looked at me. I glared at them. "You might notice that I can actually speak for myself. Ben, back off."

Ben calmed down. A little. "You sure?"

"*Yes.*"

"I'll be inside. Where I can see you." He stalked into the house and closed the door just this side of slamming it.

Jesse looked sulky. "I'm sorry."

"If you grab me again, ever, I will feed you to my dog," I said.

"I wanted to talk to you."

"Jesse, you're practically stalking me. Quit it."

"Where have you been?"

"It's not your business where I've been, but if you must know, I went to Darren Hardison's funeral."

"We were supposed to go to Rose Valley today."

"Jesse, we were not. I told you my parents wouldn't let me. And the way you acted, I wouldn't go even if they would."

"Aren't you my girl?"

Oh, God. I let my breath out in a long sigh and sat down on the steps. I patted the concrete next to me. "Jesse, sit down." He sat beside me, looking like he was waiting for the next bad thing to happen.

"Jesse, I love you. I do. But I can't handle this. You can't expect me to. I'm not even sixteen yet."

"Lots of women marry men who are older than them."

"*Marry?* Jesse, I can't think that far ahead. You can't ask me to. We have to slow down."

Jesse looked at me earnestly. "When you're twenty, I'll be twenty-four. That's not too old, that's just normal."

"It's not normal now," I said.

"Why not? Do you have another boyfriend?"

"What?"

"It's that Michalski kid, isn't it?"

"Jesse, quit it!"

"Is it because of my leg?"

"No!"

"Then what is it?" He leaned really close to me, so close I could smell his cologne. He'd put on cologne before he came to see me. That made me want to cry.

"You need to get well. You need to figure out why you get so mad all the time, and why you got rough with me. You made me afraid of you. I can't deal with that." I scooted a little ways away from him.

"I'll wait for you," he said.

"What?"

"I'll wait for you to finish high school. College too, if you want to."

And follow me around and go ballistic if you see me with a boy. I knew this had to stop. I said, "Jesse, you have to go now. I can't go out with you anymore. Not for a while, anyway. I'm sorry." I wanted to cry.

Jesse took my hand. He wasn't grabby this time, and he looked so sad that I let him. "Angie," he said, "I will do anything for you. If you'll be my girl, I'll always take care of you. I promise."

"Jesse, the person you need to take care of is you. What you need to do now is go have that scan and make sure you don't have a head injury." I'd been reading. One of the signs of head injury is that the person doesn't have any impulse control—what Felix said about not having good brakes. That would be Jesse.

He said, "Maybe."

"Good."

"If *you* want me to."

"No. Because you need to. Do not make this about me."

"It is about you, don't you understand? I *need* you."

I took my hand back. "Ben's going to be back out here in a minute if I don't go in."

Jesse glared at the window. "Is he okay with you?"

"What do you mean, *okay*?"

"He doesn't, like, get weird with you? I mean, I know he's not your real dad. You know, if anybody hurts you, you should tell me about it."

Oh, good. Someone else who wants to protect me from things that aren't happening. Of course, I'm clear on the fact that I haven't told anybody about what I may need protecting from, which is Jesse.

"Your mom leaves you here with him?" Jesse added.

"Ben has raised me since I was eight," I said. "He and Mom are having some problems right now, like I told you."

He nodded solemnly. "I just want you to know that I will always be here when you need me."

"I don't need you!" I snapped. I was crying now. "And you were right—you don't need me. You need *you.*" Need is a hell of a bad basis for love. Felix is right about that.

"Yes, you do," Jesse said. "I need you, and you'll need me sooner or later. We need each other. That's how it is. You'll see."

I stood up. "I have to go in." He started to say something and I said, "No, you can't come with me. Ben will have a fit. Let him cool down awhile, okay?"

I thought he wasn't going to go, but he finally did. I watched him till I was sure he wasn't coming back. When he turned the corner across from St. Thomas's, I went inside.

Ben wasn't even pretending he hadn't been watching the whole time. "I did not like that," he said.

"I'll handle it."

"I'm not sure that's the best idea."

"Can I just eat dinner?" I asked. "He's not coming back tonight, and Wuffie will have me up early tomorrow for church. I just want to think some, please?"

Ben let it go at that, but I know I'm going to have to figure out what to do about Jesse, or let Ben and Mom take over, and I can't bear to get him in trouble. He's right—I do love him. And he's not a monster and they'll try to make him look like one, even though he's just a kid who got sent off to shoot people and got his leg blown off. If anyone is surprised he's a little crazy, I can't imagine why. There's got to be a way to persuade him to have that scan. I feel like I'm watching that cat in the road again.

The trees were on fire. It was so hot I could feel it on my face, and it looked as if the whole sky was boiling in an orange-red bloom. The gunship stitched back and forth like a black wicked bird in front of the fire. Someone was calling, "Doc!"

I said, "I'm not Doc," trying really hard not to be this time, like Helen had said. One part of me remembered that, and I felt as if I could almost slide out of the mud and the stinking clothes I was wearing into my real body. But the body I was in was already crawling toward the wounded kid.

Be in the movie, Helen said. *Tell yourself you're dreaming.*

"Doc!" The boy was trying to crawl too, pushing himself along with his right arm. White bone stuck out of the red wreck of his other one. I pulled a tourniquet out of my bag.

I'm dreaming. I thought it hard.

"It's okay, kid, I got him."

I heard the voice in my head, and the body I had been in just crawled out from under me, and I was standing there in my pajamas. He looked back over his shoulder at me, and it was Felix. He was younger, but it was him. He wrapped the tourniquet around the stump of that torn-off arm, then pulled out a morphine Syrette and said, "Call in the dust-off chopper for me."

I didn't know how to, in my pajamas. I tried to tell him that but then I saw the chopper coming in, dark gray with a big red cross on its side. It was zig-zagging through the smoke to avoid the incoming fire and I thought it was going to crash. Then it settled with a lurch on the edge of the rice field. Felix picked up the wounded kid and ran for the chopper, splashing through the water. He ducked down under the rotors to hand him up. I could feel their wind but not the ground I was standing on, like I was only half in that place now.

I could hear, though. Shells were whining in, making an ear-shattering scream just before they exploded. The fire roared in the trees.

Felix ran back to me from the chopper as it lifted off. His face was covered in mud and his hands were bloody. He looked right at me. "Get out of here!" he said. "I've got it covered."

I opened my eyes and I was back in my bed. But I could still smell smoke, even stronger now.

20

I stumbled into the dawn half-light in the living room just as Ben and Grandma Alice came out of their rooms, their hair all sticking up on end, Ben in his boxer shorts and Grandma Alice in a long flannel nightie.

When I opened the front door, we could smell the smoke even more, enough to make your eyes water. It wasn't quite all the way light yet, but we could see black clouds boiling up into the sky over Ayala Avenue. The flames lit them up from underneath, and it was way too much like my dream.

"Oh, no!" Grandma Alice said. "What is it?"

And Ben said, "It looks like the church."

I ran across the yard in my bare feet and pajamas while Ben shouted at me to come back. I didn't listen. It did look like the smoke was coming from St. Thomas's, and what if Father Weatherford had let Felix go back and he was in the basement?

It was cold and there were lots of prickly leaves under the live oaks by the library, but I didn't pay any attention to them. I could hear sirens in the distance now, like the noises in my dream, but they were way far away. I ran past the library and across Ayala Avenue, and Felix was there, but he was all right. He was dragging a hose out of the shed and trying to screw it on the faucet in the garden. I held it for him while he got it on. He didn't even ask me what I was doing there.

We hauled the hose across Felix's herb beds and turned it on the church. Flames were shooting out of the basement window and it was so hot my face burned. The glass had broken and the wooden window frame was charred. All that black smoke we'd seen was coming out of the window and boiling up through the beams of the pergola above it, blackening the bougainvillea. You could see the leaves curling as they caught fire. Felix had the garden hose on full blast, but it wasn't doing much good.

More people had come running up, most of them just standing there watching. Ben came panting up beside me and grabbed me by the arm. I was glad to see he'd stopped to put on clothes.

"Get back and leave it to the fire department!" He dragged me to the far end of the garden, away from anything that might fall on us.

The fire truck was parking on the street and the guys

were reeling out the hose, but I could see flames coming out of the first floor windows now, at the back where the acolytes get dressed.

"Anybody know how it started?" one of the fire guys yelled as he ran past with his hose. I thought about that hot plate in the basement, but I didn't say anything. Father Weatherford's car screeched up and parked behind the fire truck. Father Weatherford came flying out, in pajamas too. He tried to go in the front door and the fire crew wouldn't let him.

"Is anyone inside?" one of them shouted at him.

He shook his head, but I know he was thinking about the statues of St. Thomas and Our Lady, plus the stained glass windows and the murals and all the other beautiful, holy things in there.

Half the town was crowding around now, getting in the way and giving the fire crew advice. Noah Michalski, who lives a few blocks away like me, was there, but he actually had some sense. He dragged another hose through the hedge from the hotel next door and started squirting it on the pergola. The pergola is big and heavy, with huge old beams in its roof. The beams near the basement window were starting to smoke, and the bougainvillea was on fire. Felix had turned his garden hose on the shed roof, which is shingle, not tile like the rest of the church. The fire in the basement was still belching smoke but no flames now, and the fire crew was working on the first floor.

Then I saw Jesse. I don't know what he was doing there. He lives at the other end of town. He ran up to me, coughing, and said, "I told you I'd be there for you." He was carrying two big buckets, and before I could say anything, he started running back and forth through the hedge, lurching on his artificial leg, dipping water out of the hotel swimming pool next door and coming back to fling it at the basement window.

"Hey man, get out from under there!" Noah yelled at him.

Jesse didn't pay any attention to him. He was coughing harder in the smoke and his face was black with soot and all scratched from the hedge. You could see the beams of the pergola glowing through the smoke.

"Jesse!" I screamed at him. He just shook his head at me and went back to running back and forth, throwing water at the window.

I'd never been so scared before. The fire looked just like a medieval picture of hell, and the air was so thick with ash and smoke that my throat burned. The fire guys were pushing through the front doors with their hoses, and they all had respirators on. The church is made out of adobe and the roof is tile, but whatever was on fire in the basement had obviously burned up through the floorboards or the wooden stairs. It would have had plenty to work on in the basement, with all the junk that's stored down there, including the hay bales left over from the Posadas parade.

Outside, Felix was still wetting down the shed. He looked just like the statue, in that awful old bathrobe all covered with soot. As I watched him, the bathrobe went away and the young guy from my dream was there, in army fatigues and combat boots, and the tree line behind him was boiling with fire. The air smelled like diesel fuel and burned meat. I blinked and it changed back again, and so did he.

This fire smelled awful anyhow, like burning wool and electrical cords and wet ashes, and my eyes stung like anything. It was getting really hard to breathe in the smoke, and people were starting to back away. Noah was still wetting the pergola down, but the fire had charred nearly through the end by the basement window. I know that when fire gets inside of wood, water on the outside doesn't put it out.

When Noah saw Jesse under that end again, he dropped his hose and ran through the smoke after him. "Get *out* of there! That's gonna come down!"

Jesse pushed Noah away, hard. Jesse's hands were all burned and his jeans were covered with ash.

Someone on the fire crew saw Jesse now and grabbed him by the arm. "Stand back, please!" It was a woman's voice, and even though I was so scared, my head stopped watching the fire long enough to think how weird it is that you can never tell who's inside those suits. And then as soon as she turned her back, Jesse picked up the buckets again.

Ben had let go of me, and I ran close enough to the pergola to yell, "Jesse, come away from there!" For an instant I thought I saw the Virgin, crying, with her hands filled with roses, and then I thought I saw Char Man. I remembered Jesse's sergeant in the Humvee, and I knew Jesse was afraid of the fire and also that it was why he wouldn't leave it. "*Jesse!*"

He stopped for a moment and looked at me again

through the smoke. Then he ran back to the window, and the whole pergola came down on top of him.

———

I just got back from the hospital. Jesse's dead. I don't know what else I can say but that. When I think about it, it all whirls around in my head like a horror movie until I throw up.

———

And I can't not think about it. All the fire crew and EMT guys were at the church. They got him out from under the beams as fast as they could, but a beam had come down right on his head, and another on his chest. Ben and Felix and Noah and I all followed the ambulance to the hospital, with Father Weatherford in his car, and waited for Jesse's mother and father to come. Father Weatherford didn't know the Francises, but I gave him their phone number and he called them.

When something really bad is going on, the hospital puts you in a separate room to wait, and all I could think about was how many other people had sat in that room waiting to find out something awful. I couldn't stand to think about Jesse except to keep praying he was okay, over and over. *Let him be okay, let him be alive, let him be okay, please let him be okay.* Let two and two not be four.

Noah's hands were burned, too, from when he tried to

haul Jesse out before the fire guys did. Ben and Felix were half waiting for Jesse's parents and half kind of hovering around both of us, making sure the kids were okay, I guess. When my stomach started to growl, Felix went and got us muffins from the hospital cafeteria, and Ben got Noah ice for his hands and some ibuprofen. The doctors were too busy with Jesse to even look at Noah. My muffin tasted like wood shavings. I couldn't eat it. I feel like I'll never want to eat anything again. I think this is why people take drugs.

Finally Jesse's parents came in. His mother looked like she was in a coma, just walking around by reflex. Father Weatherford went up and talked to them and stayed with them while they sat in those green plastic chairs and stared at the floor, holding hands. We waited two hours while they worked on him. Doctors came out a couple of times, but all they could say was they were trying to stabilize him, whatever that means. I asked Ben and he said it means heart and blood pressure and breathing, just generally the body trying to keep going. I thought about the doctors and nurses trying to keep a live person from slipping over the edge into a dead one, and what that must be like.

When the doctor came out the last time and told Jesse's parents that he was dead, I thought his mother was going to faint. But she didn't. She said, "Go tell his friends, please. I can't," and sent the doctor over to us. How do emergency room doctors bear this?

Afterward, while Father Weatherford was still talking to Jesse's parents, a nurse came out and took Noah back with her to get his hands cleaned and bandaged. They needed somebody to give them permission to treat him, so he had to call his mom. I could hear through his cell phone, she was so upset. She made it down to the hospital before he came back out of the treatment room.

"He tried to pull Jesse out from the fire," I told her.

"Oh, my God." She put her face in her hands. And then she went over to Jesse's mom and put her arms around her.

I've never seen Noah look the way he looked. Like the world had all of a sudden gotten serious and he was trying to figure it out. He could have been killed, too. As it was, his hands looked like mittens when they brought him back out—gauze bandages up to the elbows.

Jesse's dad came up to Noah and thanked him, and I thought Noah was going to cry. His mom took him home, and the nurses made Felix go back and get checked out too. They looked at me, but I told them I was fine. Felix's robe was half burned up and when he came back out, he wasn't wearing it. I think they must have taken it away from him and thrown it out. He had some gauze around one wrist but otherwise he was okay.

Father Weatherford drove Ben and me and Felix back. The seats of his car were covered with ash where we'd sat coming out, and I realized my pajamas were covered with it. No wonder the nurses looked at me.

They dropped Ben and me off at home. Ben got on the phone to Mom and I took a shower. Now I'm in bed again, like Mom, even though it's the middle of the day. I am not going to get up.

21

Mom came over later. She put her arms around me and we both cried. Her face was all red and scrunched up.

"I'm so sorry, Angie." She wiped her eyes and got a tissue from the nightstand and wiped mine. "Do you want me to go to the funeral with you? We'll all go."

"I'm not going to any more funerals."

Mom sniffled. "Don't you think it would make his parents feel better if you went?"

What could possibly make his mother feel better? I propped myself up in bed. "My stomach hurts."

"It won't be for a few days, honey."

"I'm not going anywhere. Not even out of this bed."

Mom sat back and looked at me. "I don't model very rational behavior, do I?"

"It doesn't matter." I lay back down and pulled the sheet up. I keep seeing Char Man in my head. He's all burned and he's out there waiting for everybody I love. I'm afraid to move because someone else will die. Jesse died because he was trying to prove he loved me, but I knew he did. If I lie absolutely still, maybe I won't hurt anyone else.

On Monday, I was still in bed. Helen came to see me. I think Mom or Ben must have called her. She didn't bring Lily—she came by herself and sat down in the chair by my desk while the Todal stuck his head in her lap and drooled on her. She didn't say anything, just waited for me to talk. That kind of thing drives me nuts, so finally I said, "I'm scared."

"I'm not surprised."

That wasn't what I was expecting. "Aren't you supposed to tell me not to be afraid?"

"After everything that's happened lately?" Helen scooted her chair closer to the bed. "Mental health isn't about not being afraid. Anyone who isn't afraid of anything is crazy. Mental health is about dealing with being afraid."

"Oh." I thought about that. "Helen, was Jesse crazy?"

"I never talked to him, sweetie. I don't know."

"Noah told him to get away from the fire, and so did one of the firefighters. So did I, but he didn't pay any attention to any of us."

"What do you think would make him do that?" Helen the counselor.

"I think he wanted to save my church for me," I whispered. "I think it's my fault."

"It isn't your fault when someone else is irrational." Helen was still patting the Todal. "Jesse had post-traumatic stress disorder. I think that much was clear. And probably a latent brain injury. It's possible he'd lost his ability to evaluate a situation. He'd been following orders for so long, poor boy. He may have simply heard an order in his head and followed it."

"I still don't think he would have if it weren't for me," I said.

"Maybe not," Helen said gently. "Probably not, even." She didn't ask me any more about it, but I expect she can figure it out. "But that was his doing, not yours. You can't wear everyone else's irrationality on your shoulders. You have to let people be who they are, even when they're damaged."

"Easy for you to say." I sat up some, and the Todal came over and drooled on me instead. I put my arms around his neck like he was a giant stuffed animal. "I can't quit thinking about him. Can't you give me a prescription for something that will make me quit thinking about him?"

"No, darling, I'm not a psychiatrist. But I'm going to give you a prescription to go back to school tomorrow. And another one to let yourself mourn for Jesse. Quit trying to decide whose fault it is, and let the sadness come, and sit with it. It won't go away until you do."

"What do I do about being afraid?"

Helen stood up. "Accept that the universe is an apparently random dance. There may be a pattern to it—I think there probably is—but we can't see it from where we are. You have to let the dance happen. You'll love some of it and hate some of it."

"What if I just say I'm not going to dance?"

"Then the dance will come to you. All that happens if you try to sit it out is you get bored and lonely." She bent down and kissed the top of my head. "Lily says she'll pick you up for school tomorrow."

"To make sure I go?"

She smiled. "Mmm hmm."

———

"Okay, Arnaz, rise and shine."

I opened one eye and Lily was standing at the foot of my bed, hands on her hips. She had a barbecue skewer stuck through her hair this time. Sometimes I think she looks for weird stuff to put it up with.

"I don't think I can."

"Sure you can," Lily said. "For one thing, if you don't, everyone in school will talk about you."

"I don't care."

"Good for you. Okay, you should go because your grades still matter."

"It's the beginning of the semester."

Lily sat down on the bed. "You should go because if you don't, all you'll do is lie here and think about everything being your fault, and how the whole world is going to hell in a chicken basket, and how you might as well eat worms."

I sat up then, but I said, "Maybe I want to feel that way."

She pulled the covers off me. "That's why I'm not going to let you. Besides, I have orders from Wellness Woman."

I got out of bed. When she put it that way, it just seemed more depressing to stay in bed and keep thinking. I feel so sad, but Helen said to dance, so I guess I'll dance.

"I miss him too," Lily said. "But you can do this."

─────────

School was weird, and nearly as awful as I was afraid of. All anyone can talk about is Jesse, and they keep asking me what he was really like. I'm now some kind of expert on Jesse. I hate it. Noah was nice. His hands are all bandaged, but he came anyway. And when some senior boy asked me if Jesse was crazy, Noah told him to sod off and he'd pound him if he didn't, and the senior actually backed off. Lily stuck with me all day and drove me over to St. Thomas's afterward to help clean up.

The church is a mess. Everything is scorched and smells like smoke. The fire didn't burn through the adobe walls, but the whole inside of the basement is burned out, and so is the choir office and the parish offices upstairs in the back. Even the sanctuary up front where the fire didn't get to is black with soot. Everyone is grateful that it didn't burn, but it's going to take forever to clean all the paint and gilding on the altarpiece. Father Weatherford says it needed cleaning anyway, and there was never enough money, but now people are sending in donations and it will be really beautiful. Father Weatherford is such an optimist—he reminds me of the old joke about the kid who gets a pile of horse manure for his birthday and is happy because he thinks there must be a pony somewhere.

Mom came over a bit later, and Ben and Grandpa Joe came too. I guess Felix must have been there all day.

"Ah, man, this breaks my heart," Ben said, looking around.

Mom kind of cocked her head at him, like she was thinking. Then she just said, "Come help me with the vestments. I want to see what we can save." He followed her into the back room.

If I wasn't depressed already, I would get depressed just looking at the church. The fire started in the basement, as much as anyone can tell, and all the junk down there burned, and then the fire melted a piece of plastic water pipe (which should *not* have been installed in plastic pipe, according to everybody, but nobody knows who did it), and that flooded the whole basement. So everything that isn't burned is wet and rotting, and a lot of it is both.

But I don't care if Father Weatherford is a goof who is always looking for a pony, because he did something that made me want to kiss him. Everybody—meaning the Parish Council and the Altar Society—was telling each other how they'd told him so, and "that man," meaning Felix, "should never have been allowed to stay in the basement, and we said over and over that he was dangerous." This right where Felix could hear them while he carried load after load of wet horrible stuff out of the basement, stuff *they* weren't going to touch. And he wasn't staying there the night of the fire, but they were going to blame him anyway.

And Father Weatherford called everybody together and said, "We don't have the fire department's report yet, but I am afraid that I'm responsible."

"Now, Father, you always have such faith in people, you mustn't blame yourself when it's misplaced." That was Mrs. Beale, the Altar Society nut with the flashlight who found me in the basement with Felix.

"No, Mrs. Beale, I mean that I am directly responsible for the fire." Father Weatherford looked so tired and miserable, all covered with soot. "The fire department thinks it could have been a short in the wiring, and I fear that I caused it. The fuses in the basement have been blowing nearly every time we turn the lights on, and there didn't seem to be any reason for it. I was getting very tired of stumbling down in the dark to change them and I remembered my grandfather telling me about a trick of putting a penny in the fuse. So I tried that."

And that's apparently a very bad idea. The way Ben explained it to me, the penny keeps the fuse from blowing and that lets the wire heat up so much it can make sparks shoot out of an outlet, so even if it's inside an adobe wall, it can spit sparks out at the stack of hay bales you just happen to have left near the outlet.

"I'm afraid that the heater in the basement was still switched on," Father said, "and I never thought to check it. I can't blame anyone but myself for that. I should have seen that the fuses were a sign something wasn't right. So I must ask you to lay the blame for this tragedy at my door. All I can do, in turn, is offer my penitence to God."

Everybody got very quiet after that, and nobody said anything else about Felix.

22

Jesse's funeral was Wednesday at the Presbyterian church, and I did go after all. I had to say goodbye to him. Mom came with me, and so did Ben. They both looked like they were about to cry and they actually sat together. Felix came, in the good clothes he'd worn to Wuffie's for Christmas. Lily and her parents were there, and Noah and his mom, and lots and lots of people from school. I wish Jesse could have seen how many people came. Noah sat down beside me and whispered, "You okay?"

I nodded. He was trying to turn the pages in the hymn-book with bandages on his hands. I turned them for him. "Do they still hurt?" I asked. They looked like they did.

"Not so bad. Built-in excuse for not doing homework."

"You don't do your homework anyway," I whispered

back, and he smiled at me. Then the smile faded out when Jesse's mom and dad went past us down the aisle with his little brother and sister. "Dude, I tried to get him out of there," Noah said to me.

"I know you did."

The minister talked about how brave Jesse was, and dedicated to serving others, and I hope it made his mom feel better. But I still don't know what could.

We didn't have to go to the cemetery afterward because Jesse's parents had him cremated, and now he's in a little niche in the church wall. I want to go and talk to him through the bricks, but I don't know what to say.

———

Thursday we were back at school again, and then after school I went back to St. Thomas's. There weren't so many people as on the first couple of days, but Mom and Ben and Grandpa Joe are all still showing up. Mrs. Beale, who really is a total idiot, thanked Ben and Grandpa Joe over and over again and kept saying how nice it was of them to come, since they're Jewish.

Grandpa Joe finally got fed up with her, I think, because he said, "No problem. You're probably all Marranos anyway."

She looked like she wasn't sure what he'd just called her, and he said, "You don't know about the Marranos?"

Mrs. Beale said she didn't, so he explained. I didn't know either, but it turns out that Queen Isabella and King Ferdinand of Spain (yeah, the same ones who funded

Christopher Columbus) told all the Spanish Jews that they had to either convert or leave the country. So lots of them pretended to convert because if they left they couldn't take any money or property with them. But the Spanish Inquisition was always looking for *conversos* who had backslid, to torture them and burn them at the stake. So the Spanish Jews would eat pork to prove they were really converted. That's what "marrano" means. It's really kind of a rude term—it means "pork-eater" or just "pig." After a while, the descendants of the *conversos* kind of forgot they were Jews. They had funny little family habits like lighting candles on Friday nights, but they didn't know why.

"Lots of *conversos* in the New World," Grandpa Joe said. "It was a fine chance to duck the Inquisition and get the hell out of Spain. Then you forget who you are. You intermarry with some Catholics, some Indians; maybe even the odd little traditions disappear."

Mrs. Beale said, "I'm quite certain that's not the case in my family. But how interesting." She looked like she was sucking a prune.

"Oh, lots of them took new names," Grandpa Joe said. He sounded like he was having way too good a time with this. "I've read that if your surname is the name of a Spanish city, you're probably a Marrano. Like Burgos, or Zaragoza."

Mrs. Beale, whose daughter married Bill Zaragoza and is raising lots of little Zaragozas, looked really ticked now. Wuffie must have heard them because she came swooping over and said, "Joe, help me with this ladder, please," and practically dragged him off by the hair.

But I'm hanging on to that idea. Wuffie's descended from one of the Spanish colonial families, and I hope we *are* Marranos. Those people held on to who they really were through all those generations, lighting candles on Friday night and saying prayers they couldn't understand. Even if they didn't know what it was all about anymore, they still had it. I only have Mom's side of my family, because I don't know anything about my real father besides his name. Grandpa Joe's family are Ashkenazi, Jews from Europe. But Ben's family are Sephardic Jews, like from Spain and the Middle East, so if we really are Marranos, then I feel like I have a connection to Ben, too.

I like the idea of everybody being connected like that, in all these mysterious, hidden ways, like traveling through secret tunnels. And maybe Gil Arnaz was one. Could be.

We went on cleaning up, washing the soot off the walls and shoveling out the disgusting crud in the basement. When stuff gets wet, it just rots. Sometimes you can't even tell what it used to be. It's like glop. But back under all the glop, I found the statue. I think.

It's hard to tell, because all I found is a chunk of wood and it's really burned, and then it was sitting in water for days (there was about a foot of revolting water on the floor, and they had to pump it out before we could even start to clean up). Not to mention we had to shut off all the electricity to the basement. They set up some spotlights that shone down the stairs until someone could check the wiring. But in the far back storeroom, I found this thing that's the right size. I think I can sort of see his face, or where it used to be.

I also swear it was not in that room before. So I went looking for Felix to show it to him, and he wasn't there.

For some reason that gave me the creeps, so I went to the park to look for him. His tent is still set up, but there's no one in it. I went back to the church and asked Father Weatherford, and Mom, and anyone else I saw, and none of them know where he's gone, either. Everybody kept saying, "Well, I just saw him," but nobody can find him.

Now I can't get the idea out of my head that Felix and the statue really are connected some way, and something has happened to him.

By that time it was dark out and I didn't know where else to look, so I went home with Ben. And Mom came too, surprise! Grandma Alice had made dinner, and we all sat down to eat just as if Mom still lived here. I have no idea what she thinks she's doing, or Ben either, but she was still here when I went to bed—in Ben's office with him, doing their income taxes! I heard her car start up about midnight, so she didn't stay the night.

I went to sleep worrying about Felix and hoping it wouldn't make me have any of his dreams. Instead, I dreamed that Jesse wasn't really dead; it was all a mistake. I kept saying to him, "We have to tell people, they're all crying." Then I woke up and remembered, and cried myself. But I wish I knew where Felix is. I am not going to be able to stand it if anyone else dies.

————

In the morning, Ben was still in his clothes from the day before and he hadn't shaved. He was making waffles, which is my favorite breakfast.

He said, "Grab the syrup, Angelfish," and plopped a plate down in front of me.

I said, "You look awful."

"Up all night."

"What were you doing?" I know it wasn't shagging Mom, because I heard her car leave, but he looked cheerful.

"Fixing a script."

"All night? Fixing it how?"

"Just something Sylvia thought didn't work."

Then it dawned on me. "You took out whatever it was she was mad at you about using?"

"Sometimes how someone feels about something is more important than whether they're right," Ben said. "So she's still wrong, but I took it out anyway."

I stabbed a forkful of waffle. "What was it?"

Ben grinned at me. "If Sylvia doesn't want it in my script, I'm pretty sure she doesn't want me to tell you about it, either."

"Are you getting back together?" I asked.

"Plans will be announced."

They are. I know they are. And it didn't have anything at all to do with me, or Felix interceding, or anything else except them. They had to work out their own stuff, and I will never have any idea at all how they did it. It would make a very lousy movie—no role for the precocious teenage daughter.

And I'm happy about it and all, but somehow it seems

like an anticlimax. I still don't know where Felix is, and I'm so sad over Jesse that I think my heart will break. I guess that's what Helen meant about the dance.

———

Then at school I heard the worst thing. The fire department found some evidence of arson, and they don't think it was Felix, thank God, but they do think it might have been Jesse. It was all over school. In a small town, everyone always knows everything. Even if they get it wrong. But I'm really afraid they don't have this wrong.

After lunch, a guy from the fire department was even at school interviewing people. They called me into the principal's office to talk to him. He was a big guy with a buzz cut and hands the size of suitcases, but he seemed nice.

He said, "I'm Lieutenant Shaw. I understand you were a good friend of Jesse Francis."

I nodded. My stomach felt crawly.

"You could say, maybe, he was romantically interested in you?"

"He's—he was lots older," I managed to say.

"Did he ever say he would do something to impress you? Be a hero for you?"

"He already lost his leg in the army," I said. "How much more of a hero?"

Lieutenant Shaw looked unhappy, but he kept poking at it. "Sometimes, when young men like girls, they look for ways to impress them, maybe do something heroic for the girl. Sometimes they don't think it through very well."

I didn't say anything. Lieutenant Shaw said, "Did Jesse Francis ever say anything like that to you? Like, 'I'd do anything for you'? Things like that?"

I thought about Jesse saying, "I told you I'd be there for you," and carrying those buckets. He doesn't—didn't—even live at our end of town. How did he happen to be there with buckets? I thought about Felix and how he might have gotten blamed instead, or been in the church and been trapped. Then I thought about Jesse's mother.

"No, I don't think he ever did," I said.

"You do realize that more people could have died?" Lt. Shaw said. "And that my crew could have been killed trying to save a historic landmark?"

I nodded. But I don't see what difference it makes now. Jesse's dead. I'm not going to help them prove he did it when all it will accomplish is make his mother feel even worse, if that's possible.

They sent me back to class, and I've been thinking about this ever since. It's not fun to think someone might have done something like that for you. If that's love, it's a very scary kind. Not the kind I ever want.

I thought I might have nightmares about it. But I didn't dream at all, which scared me even worse, because where has Felix gone? I'd be happy now if he showed up in a dream, even.

And I never thought I would say this, but I want my mother.

23

He's at Wuffie's house. I got Ben to drop me off on the way to his Saturday tennis game, and Felix was sitting on the floor clipping Cookie's toenails.

"Where have you *been*?"

Cookie gave me a popeyed look and started drooling. I lowered my voice. "I was worried about you."

"As you can see, I'm all here."

I thought, *I wouldn't bet on that*, but I didn't say it. I told him I found the statue, and he gave me this look and said, "Well, I guess I can't go back in there."

"No, it's pretty much of a mess," I said sarcastically. Now that I wasn't panicking, I was mad at him for scaring me. "You might want to inhabit St. Thomas instead."

"Oh, I don't think *he* would let me in." Felix snipped off the last toenail and Cookie sat up. He fed her a biscuit.

"I do not believe in any of this," I said, despite the fact that I *had* half believed it when I couldn't find him.

"I used to think God might take me back," Felix said. "But it doesn't look like he's going to. I'll have to figure out something else. Maybe it's time I gave up the sainthood thing. Settled down."

"Absolutely," I said. "Sensible thing to do."

He scratched Cookie's ears. "The Virgin says I should hit the road, see what I find."

All of a sudden I didn't care what he was. I just didn't want him to leave. "That's not settling down! Why?"

"Check out who else I am," he said. "Since I seem to be stuck here."

"How am I going to get along without you? Who am I going to talk to?"

"I think you can probably talk to yourself now," he said.

I think maybe I probably can. But it feels like having somebody else die.

Felix looked like he knew that. "You still having my dreams?"

"Not since the fire," I told him. "And that one was even freakier than the others. You were in it too, and you talked to me."

He nodded like he remembered. "I don't think you'll have them anymore."

"How do you know?"

"I told 'em to stick with me."

"You *want* them?"

"I don't mind them. They're kind of like friends now."

"How can you make dreams listen to you?" This conversation was getting as weird as talking to Felix always did, like he was getting some kind of transmission from a mother ship nobody else can tune in to.

"I had to tell them it was okay, let them come home."

That halfway made sense.

He reached into a pocket of his shirt and pulled out something wrapped up in a scrap of cloth. "I made you something. Since I ruined your statue."

He put it in my hand and I unwound it. It was a little *santo*, carved out of wood. It might have been the Virgin with a crown of roses on her head. Or it could have been a man with a robe and tonsure. It was hard to tell.

"So you'll have somebody to talk to," he said. "From your lips to their ears."

"'Their ears?'"

"There are lots of people listening to you, you just don't see them all."

Saints from the eighth dimension, maybe. I remembered what Helen said about the pattern of the universe. I think that looking at it from where we are, we might as well all be dyslexic. There are probably a lot of things we just don't see, or see backwards. Cupcake came and put her head in Felix's lap beside Cookie's. I watched him snuggling the spaniels and thought about him cleaning out the church anyway while all those old ladies were saying he'd started the fire.

"Grandpa Joe told me about something when I was little," I told him. "It's called *tikkun olam*. That's Hebrew for mending the world. I think that's what you do."

He ducked his head. "Not me."

"Not the big things," I said. "Not global warming or AIDS or things like that. What one person can do. Mending the things you can mend. Taking care of Cookie. Planting lavender. Being kind to people."

"Little stuff?" he said.

"Little stuff. Just whatever we can do. If you do that, you mend those boys you couldn't save, too, I think." I was starting to sound like Felix, but I really did think so. I still do. I'm not sure he can mend himself, but he mends other people.

He didn't say anything. His head was still bent over and now I saw tears on his face. I leaned down and kissed his bald spot. Or his tonsure. "Is Mom around?"

"She's out back."

I went through the kitchen and out the back door to the vegetable garden, where Mom was watering the romaine. We haven't had any rain yet. It's really wonderful when it rains. The hills turn green overnight and then they're covered with yellow mustard flowers and orange poppies, like somebody poured paint out of a bucket. Right now everything is still brown.

Mom was setting a sprinkler on the lettuce. She turned the faucet on and it jetted around and shot me in the face.

I backed out of range while the sprinkler whirred its way across the garden.

"Sorry about that!" Mom called.

"Can I talk to you?" I dodged the sprinkler and sat down on the rock wall.

Mom sat down next to me. "What is it?"

"Felix is leaving." I kicked the wall.

"I know, honey. Wuffie asked him to stay here and do the stuff that Grandpa Joe is getting too old to do, but he won't. I think he wants to see if he can make it on his own."

"I can't stand it."

She put her arm around me. "You can stand what you have to stand."

"Are you coming back home?"

She smiled. "Yeah."

"I'm glad about that."

"I want you to be very clear that I'm glad you're glad, but also that I'm not doing it for you. No one should make or leave a marriage for anyone else's sake."

"Got that," I said.

"Well, remember it," Mom said. She squeezed my shoulders.

"Mom, why did you marry my dad?"

She got real quiet then. She didn't take her arm away but she sat absolutely still for three minutes, which is a long time. I timed it, counting hippopotamuses the way you do to scald a tomato. I could have scalded a whole bushel.

Finally she said, "For all the reasons I just told you why you *shouldn't* make a marriage. Because he wanted me to. Because I was afraid no one else would want me again. Because I wanted children. Because I wanted a second chance at getting love right."

"With a South American gangster you met in a bar? Honestly, Mom."

"That's Wuffie's version. He wasn't South American, and I met him in a library. Wuffie didn't like him, but I was old enough to do what I wanted, so they gave me a big wedding and prayed."

"Were you pregnant?"

"No, but I wanted to be."

"Why did you leave him?"

"I didn't. He left me."

Oh. That might explain a lot.

"I was pregnant then," Mom went on, "and I was way too demanding. He had business to take care of, and I thought I could get him to change. Instead, one day he was just gone. He left me you, though." Another long pause. "Do you want to look for him?"

I knew she was hoping I didn't, but she'd let me if I wanted to. I've thought about it before, but by now I'm pretty sure Ben's the only father I really want. "Sometime, maybe. When I'm eighteen." When nobody can get any insane custody ideas. I don't think I would trust Gil Arnaz. "For, like, his medical history," I said. "Not now. It's just that I don't understand guys and I thought maybe there was some secret password, you know, handed down from mother to daughter with the tampons talk, that you'd for-gotten to tell me."

Mom kind of snorted. "Boy, are you talking to the wrong person."

I sighed. "Okay, how about your first husband? The one who gave you the rabbit?"

Mom looked wistful at that. "Brian Reilly." She shook her head. "He was seventeen and I was sixteen and we swore eternal love at a football game. His family was going to move to Ohio as soon as school let out, so after the game we took his dad's car to Las Vegas and got married."

"Were you drunk?" I asked. Maybe that wasn't tactful, but I want to know what makes people do things.

"Only on the romance of it all. Then we woke up in a motel room that had bedbugs because that was all we could afford, and I knew we'd been stupid. I wouldn't admit that to Wuffie, but I knew. I was tragic about it, but I let her get the marriage annulled."

That struck me as so sad. "Do you still think about him?"

"No, sweetie, not really. I feel bad because maybe I messed up his life—when you're seventeen you've got a grown-up body and a baby brain, and it's so hard. I worry about what an awful example I've set for you."

"I have no plans to elope," I assured her. "I'd really like to make the first marriage work out."

"Like I said, you aren't talking to the right person. Ask Wuffie. She's been married to Grandpa for forty-seven years."

"No way." I am so not going to ask my grandmother about sex. And I suspect Mom really knows more than

Wuffie. Mom probably knows what I need to know. "But, Mom—"

"Yeah?"

I bit my lip. "Well, Jesse was at the fire? And he tried to put it out?"

"Angela, please don't speak to me in questions."

"Sorry." I made myself quit that. But it's so easy to do when you're feeling unsure of yourself, like it kind of protects you from what you're actually saying. "Well, Jesse was there right away and now the fire department thinks it wasn't the fuses after all. They think he set the fire, to impress me by putting it out."

Mom let out a long sigh.

"You think so too?" I demanded.

"Helen Reinder said it wouldn't surprise her," Mom said. "I'm pretty sure you were more serious with Jesse than you've told me."

"Mom, how can someone do something totally horrible because he loves you?"

"I never did figure that out," Mom said. "But I did figure out that people don't do things like that from real love. Out of obsessive love maybe. Or they're using you as an excuse. But not real love. That's not the way real love behaves."

"Real love takes a plot point out of a script even when he still thinks you're wrong?"

"Yeah." Mom smiled. "For the record, I'm not wrong."

"You're not ever going to tell me what it was, are you?"

Mom took a deep breath. "You know, I think I will."

"You're kidding."

But she wasn't. She told me.

She kept her arm around me while she talked. "Have you ever had anything happen to you that was just so humiliating and awful that you cringed every time you thought about it, even a long time afterward?"

Okay, I can relate to that. "Yeah," I said.

"Well, this was one of those. It's been thirty years, and it still made my stomach knot up. But it's odd, now—after Darren and Jesse dying, it suddenly seems so far away, it's just not worth hiding anymore."

"Is this about First Husband?" I still wondered if she'd been pining for him all this time.

"Yeah. I told you, I realized the next morning that we'd been stupid. There we were, in this awful motel room with bedbugs and a stopped-up toilet, and I just knew that our whole life was going to be like that because there was no way we were old enough to be grownups. I called Wuffie while he was in the bathroom, and it made him so angry. He said I didn't love him and we started to argue, and then it got into a shouting match and he called me a whore and drove off and left me there."

"Oh my God."

"He was hurt. I'd made him feel like a fool. I can see that now. But the motel owner heard him and thought I really was a prostitute, and he threw me out. I had to sit on the sidewalk in my best dress, that I'd gotten married in, all stained and torn where I'd caught my heel in it, and wait for Wuffie and Grandpa Joe to come and get me. It took hours, and every so often the motel owner would stick his head out the door and yell at me and threaten to call the police, but I didn't have any money or any way to call my parents again and I'd told them where I'd be and I was afraid to leave for fear they wouldn't find me. I've never been so terrified."

"But they came and got you?"

"Oh yes. I knew they'd gotten in the car the minute they hung up the telephone. But it's a day's drive. It was night by the time they got there. Wuffie wanted to know why I was sitting on the sidewalk, but I was too humiliated to tell her."

"Oh God, Mom."

"Brian tried to talk to me once after I got back, but I wouldn't let him get near me. I think maybe he was sorry. But then his family moved and I never saw him again. I've always cringed inside every time I even thought about sitting in front of that motel with that man calling me a whore and people staring at me. After I went to college, I always felt different from the other girls because I'd been married, even if they didn't know about it. I never told anyone, and I don't think Brian did either."

You don't expect to hear stuff like that from your mother. I guess we're more alike than I thought. She fell in love without thinking it through, like me, and when she fell in love again, the second time, she thought she could change my dad like I thought I could fix Jesse.

"And Ben wanted to put that in a script?" No wonder she was mad. She married Ben and thought she'd finally gotten love right, and then he was so totally clueless he couldn't see what this meant to her. I said, "I love Ben, but he's a moron."

Mom smiled. She even looked kind of affectionate. "You know writers."

"You were going to go back to him even if he hadn't taken it out, weren't you?" I could tell by her expression.

"I told you, after everything that's happened, that memory just doesn't seem to make me sick anymore. It doesn't seem so poisonous, you know?"

"So why did he take it out?"

"I think he finally figured out that I wasn't mad because it embarrassed me, I was mad because I felt betrayed all over again, this time by him, when he wanted to use it and wouldn't listen to me."

"Okay," I said. "Maybe Ben isn't a moron, he's just slow on the uptake."

"What he is," Mom said, "is someone who really loves me. I'll have to settle for that."

I didn't say, *well, duh*, or anything else I might have said last week. I said, "I'm not ever going to understand Jesse, am I?"

"No, probably not," Mom said. "Jesse was way too complicated. That's what I was scared of. But at least you had some sense." She sighed. "If it had been me, I'd probably have run off with him just because someone told me I couldn't."

"Are you saying I have more sense than you do?" Not that I haven't thought so from time to time. Now, though, I'm not sure.

"Did. Past tense. But yes." Then she said, "But don't quote me on that some night when you come in after curfew and expect it to get you anywhere."

"Got it."

We sat on the wall for a while watching the sprinkler shoot little water diamonds in a circle. Then Grandpa Joe and Felix came out with three beers and an Orangina. They handed Mom a beer and me the Orangina and we all watched the sprinkler until Wuffie said lunch was ready.

24

Mom came home this morning with her suitcases, and the Todal went nuts. He knows what suitcases mean. Mommy's home! Bless us all here at the Untied Church of Dog.

Grandma Alice is so pleased to have Mom back that when we left for Mass she was fixing a roast chicken to celebrate, even though we aren't usually Sunday-dinner-in-the-middle-of-the-day people.

St. Thomas's won't be ready until Easter, so we went to Our Lady of Good Counsel and Noah and his mother were there too. The bandages are off his left hand. It looks really red, and the skin is tight—he's going to have scars—but the doctor says it's healing just fine. The right hand is worse. He still has a dressing on that one, so I fixed his punch for him afterward. He can hold a cookie though, so I refused to feed him.

"Some nurse you are," he said.

"It's all about therapy," I told him. "Force the patient to be as independent as possible." I almost cried then, since I'd been reading up on that because of Jesse. I told Noah, "It's for the sake of your self-esteem," which is actually probably not a problem for Noah.

Noah said, "You look depressed, Ange."

"I keep thinking about Jesse," I said. "And Felix took off." Nobody's seen him since lunch yesterday.

"The old dude?"

"Yeah." I looked at Noah like I dared him to say something smart-ass, but he didn't.

"He was cool, the way he got the hoses going at the fire." Noah picked at the bandage on his hand. "It was rough, what happened to Jesse. I've been feeling weird, too. Jesse was scary. He was, like, so hungry. He wanted stuff, you know, and he didn't know how to get it."

"I know."

"It's that—what do they call it when someone isn't mature?"

"Nobody ever told you?"

"Very funny. I'm *supposed* to act like I'm fifteen. Arrested development—that's what I mean. He went into the army when he was seventeen, and he never got to be a kid and fart around."

I looked at Noah sideways so he wouldn't see I was impressed. He's actually grown up a lot since last fall. I wonder if watching what happened to Jesse had something to do with it. Before Jesse, I'd have pegged Noah as someone likely to join the army at seventeen just to shoot at people.

I'm doing better too, sort of. Sometimes now I'm halfway okay, and then I remember and it's like my heart will stop. Helen says you can't rush the dance.

25

It's been two months since Felix left, but I'd still been half hoping he'd be there when we went back to St. Thomas's. He wasn't. On the other hand, Father Weatherford was right about the altarpiece. It's so lovely, it just glows. There are vines and stars in rose and deep blue and soft green on the arch over the altar, and new gilding on the sunburst at the center, and the faux marble on the columns is rose-gold now and three shades lighter than it was. There are details I never saw before—in the painting of Our Lady of Sorrows, for instance, her hands are full of roses even though there is a sword stuck through her heart.

St. Thomas is pleased, I think. At least his statue is smiling, and I have to sort of smile back even if he did say that women are defective and misbegotten. I give him the benefit of the doubt for living in the thirteenth century when no one was exactly enlightened. He also said that poets and philosophers are alike in being big with wonder, which sounds like something Felix would say. I miss Felix like mad.

It's Easter, but it's cold out. There was a late frost last night and you could hear the wind machines going all over the valley to keep the oranges from freezing. They set up funny echoes sometimes, tricks of the sound waves. I kept thinking I could hear the Underworld doors banging shut behind someone, Jesse maybe.

Or maybe just behind all our mistakes. I'd rather think of it that way. Mom and Ben are acting like they never split up, only even more cheerful. I don't think Mom's problem really is that she can't settle down—she just tried to settle down too early with Brian Reilly, and then my dad was kind of a catch-up for her. I can't imagine Mom thinking no one else would want to marry her. She gave me her poetry journal this morning and told me I could read it if I wanted to. She said this one was about the Las Vegas thing:

What I Haven't Lost Yet

More than you would think. The owner's manual
for a car that always had a demon in it
and the radio the cat peed in,
making it likely to burst out

with polka music on its own, or

a Sunday preacher promising damnation
to girls who like to mess around with girls.

Toasters missing a part, and formulas
no longer describing the circumference of a circle,
or the square of the hypotenuse.

These truncated remains keep stubborn
residence in my brain, with the Ipana toothpaste song,
and faces of boys who once betrayed me.
What we keep is not always what will stay.

I asked her if she really remembered the Ipana song, which is apparently an ancient brand of toothpaste, and she said that was actually Wuffie's memory. She said poetry is about truth, not facts. Then she sang it for me. Good God.

————

What I'm going to save of Jesse is the otter. And the way he said nobody was going to use him as a poster boy for their causes. I kept some of Jesse's drawings, too, but I gave most of them to his mother. I had so many. I expect his face will stay, too, whether I want it to or not. But that's okay.

What I have of Felix is the little statue. I keep it on my nightstand and I do talk to it. It looks like it's listening. When I was little, I thought that people were solid all the way through, like potatoes. When I learned about skeletons it scared me to death. Now I think that maybe your soul or whatever it is has all kinds of layers, too. Maybe Felix is just an extreme example of that.

He was right. You can only watch. I couldn't make Jesse okay by loving him. Or Felix either. And I'm going to have to live with that, because that's what grown-ups do. That's what Ben and Mom do, and it's no wonder it gives them trouble and they freak out. In a movie, Felix would have turned out to be a long-lost uncle and moved in with us. In a movie, *I* would have been burned in the fire and Mom and Ben would have reconciled over my hospital bed. In a movie, I would have helped Jesse get well because only I understood him. He would have run a marathon on his C-Leg and given hope to other injured soldiers, instead of trying to burn down a church to impress me.

As it is, maybe Mom and Ben will stay together and maybe they won't, and I won't be able to do a thing about it. That's kind of freeing, actually.

———————

Grandma Alice made Sunday dinner for us again. It was eggplant lasagna this time. I fed the eggplant to the Todal. Thanks be to Dog.

Acknowledgments

As always, I owe thanks to the people who have shepherded this book on its way. Particularly I have to thank Han Nolan, who read it in multiple drafts and encouraged me to get going on it; my wonderful agent Sarah Davies; my equally wonderful editors Brian Farrey and Sandy Sullivan; the art department at Flux for the coolest cover ever; my endlessly patient husband Tony Neuron; my brother-in-law Michael Neuron, for putting me on to Char Man; and Robert Campbell, who vetted the Vietnam scenes for me—any mistakes there are my own and not his.

My gratitude also goes to the students and faculty in the Graduate Program in Children's Literature at Hollins University, who heard me read bits and pieces of it at faculty readings and kindly indicated that they'd like to hear the rest of the story.

The names of four of the characters in this book belong to my son Felix and his friends Noah, Jesse, and Darren, who quite a long time ago, when they were about twelve, once said to me, "You write books? Cool! Put our names in one." So I have.

And finally, a general acknowledgement to a beloved town: Ojai, California, where I grew up and which provided the template for Ayala; and to the Ojai boys who went to war and didn't come back, or came back someone else.

About the Author

Amanda Cockrell is a native of California, daughter of a screenwriter and a novelist. She is the founding director of Hollins University's graduate program in children's literature and managing editor of the university's literary journal, *The Hollins Critic*. She has received fiction fellowships from the National Endowment for the Arts and the Virginia Commission for the Arts. At varying times she has also been a newspaper reporter and a copywriter for a rock radio station. When not otherwise occupied, she makes found-object collages, most often santos and shrines for imaginary deities.